Kylie Jean

by Marci Peschke

illustrated by Tuesday Mourning

PICTURE WINDOW BOOKS
a capstone imprint

Kylie Jean is published by Picture Window Books
A Capstone Imprint
1710 Roe Crest Drive
North Mankato, Minnesota 56003
www.capstonepub.com

Previously published as three separate editions:
Dancing Queen 978-1-4048-7209-7
Spelling Queen 978-1-4048-7212-7
Cupcake Queen 978-1-4795-6753-9

Library of Congress Cataloging-in-Publication Data is available at the Library of
Congress website.

Design Element Credit:
Shutterstock/blue67design

For Caitlyn
with love for Rick
—MP

Printed   and   bound   in   China.
004415

Kylie Jean

All About Me, Kylie Jean!

My name is Kylie Jean Carter. I live in a big, sunny, yellow house on Peachtree Lane in Jacksonville, Texas with Momma, Daddy, and my two brothers, T.J. and Ugly Brother.

T.J. is my older brother, and Ugly Brother is . . . well . . . he's really a dog. Don't you go telling him he is a dog. Okay? I mean it. He thinks he is a real true person.

He is a black-and-white bulldog. His front looks like his back, all smashed in. His face is all droopy like he's sad, but he's not.

His two front teeth stick out and his tongue hangs down. (Now you know why his name is Ugly Brother.)

Everyone I love to the moon and back lives in Jacksonville. Nanny, Pa, Granny, Pappy, my aunts, my uncles, and my cousins all live here. I'm extra lucky, because I can see all of them any time I want to!

My momma says I'm pretty. She says I have eyes as blue as the summer sky and a smile as sweet as an angel. (Momma says pretty is as pretty does. That means being nice to the old folks, taking care of little animals, and respecting my momma and daddy.)

But I'm pretty on the outside and on the inside. My hair is long, brown, and curly.

I wear it in a ponytail sometimes, but my absolute most favorite is when Momma pulls it back in a princess style on special days.

I just gave you a little hint about my big dream. Ever since I was a bitty baby I have wanted to be an honest-to-goodness beauty queen. I even know the wave. It's side to side, nice and slow, with a dazzling smile. I practice all the time, because everybody knows beauty queens need to have a perfect wave.

I'm Kylie Jean, and I'm going to be a beauty queen. Just you wait and see!

Kylie Jean

Dancing Queen

Table of Contents

Chapter One
Queen of the Crop

It's almost summertime, but this Saturday morning is cool and dewy.

My whole family — aunts, uncles, and a bunch of cousins — is at Lickskillet Farm. We're picking veggies from the huge garden patch.

Standing next to me is my best cousin, Lucy. Momma, Daddy, T.J. and Ugly Brother are here, too.

As far as I can see, row after row of green leafy tops fill the farm garden.

"Look at all these veggies," Pa crows. "This year we have a bumper crop! I'm going to have to give away carrots, peas, and greens," he adds, shaking his head. "There are just too many vegetables to can in jars or freeze for later."

I slip off my shoes and bury my feet in the soft, black dirt while Pa and Nanny decide which vegetables to pick.

Momma pulls on some red garden gloves with little green flowers. My gloves are pink, with little green flowers. Pink is my color, in case you didn't know.

Lucy fidgets and frowns. She points to the greens and says, "I sure hope we don't have to pick greens. I squish 'em every time!"

I nod. Greens are boring to pick.

Finally, Pa says, "T.J., you come with me to the cornfield. The rest of you, stay in the garden patch. My best girl can pick peas." He means my momma. He adds, "Kylie Jean and Lucy can pull carrots."

We shout, "Yippee!" Then we push a wheelbarrow down to the rows of carrots. Next to them, a scarecrow wearing one of Nanny's aprons, a hat, and some old cowboy boots dances in the breeze.

I get busy pulling carrots. That's more fun than pulling weeds! You can't eat weeds, but carrots are pretty tasty.

Suddenly, I see Ugly Brother. There's a big ole carrot hanging out of his mouth like a giant orange tongue. While we have been pulling the carrots, he has been eating them!

"Ugly Brother! Stop trying to eat all the carrots we just pulled," I shout, laughing. "They're still dirty, and you don't even like carrots!"

"Ruff," he barks. That means he doesn't want to stop eating carrots. But he moves away. Then he watches while we pick more carrots.

Some of the carrots are teeny-tiny babies, and some are giants as long as a grown-up's foot. I like the feathery green tops of the carrots best. They are so pretty, like lace on a Sunday dress.

I like picking carrots, but after a while, I get bored. Then T.J. comes over. He's here to boss me around. I just know it!

He says, "Hey, Lil' Bit, Pa told me to come help you." He frowns, looks at me, and adds, "No wonder you're so slow. You're wearin' a dress."

Putting my hands on my hips, I glare at T.J. "Hey, Lucy's wearin' a dress, too," I inform him. "We like dresses! They're not slowin' us down!"

"Let's have a picking contest," T.J. says. Then he starts pulling carrots to get a head start.

I shake my head. "No way," I tell him.

"You always win anyway!" Lucy mutters.

T.J. moves down the rows of carrots, pulling handfuls and tossing them on the ground. He is a fast carrot picker. Lucy is picking over on the next row, and she's been in the same spot ever since we got started. "You girls pick up the ones I pull out," T.J. tells us. "Then put them in the wheelbarrow."

Lucy and I look at each other. She shrugs. Neither of us wants to help T.J., but we don't have a choice.

"Okay," I say. "But we were doin' just fine before you got here."

As we pick up the carrots, Lucy asks, "Did you know that Madame Girard is planning a ballet performance of Swan Lake?"

Lucy is taking dance studio lessons from Madame Girard. Our friend Cara takes lessons there too. Momma says studio lessons are not in our budget, so I have been taking ballet classes at the Jacksonville Recreation Center for the last three months.

"Really? It sounds so pretty," I say, picturing a big white swan with a long smooth neck. "What's it about?" I ask.

Lucy says, "It's all about the beautiful Odette, Queen of the Swans, and her swan maidens. You won't believe it, but Odette and the maidens are enchanted, so by day they are swans, but at night they turn into beautiful girls. Real girls! Only a prince can break the evil spell."

I think I must be under a spell, too.

Just hearing the word queen puts me in a trance. Then an idea hits my brain like a bee on a blossom.

While Lucy watches, I make a green, lacy crown from the tops of some carrots. Then I do ballet turns down the carrot row.

T.J. rolls his eyes. He says, "Lil' Bit, how about more workin' and less dancing."

Lucy asks me, "Are you Odette?"

"Yup! I'm the swan queen," I tell her.

Suddenly, all I can think about is being Queen of the Swans.

Lucy smiles and shakes her head. She knows all about my big dream to be a beauty queen.

We see Pa's straw hat coming our way. Nanny thinks it's not fit for a scarecrow, but Pa loves that old hat.

He wants to check on us. Thanks to T.J., our wheelbarrow is so full that carrots are hanging over the sides. "Good work, kid!" he tells T.J. He gives Lucy a little squeezy hug. "I bet you helped a lot," he tells her. Lucy just grins.

Then he looks at me. I'm still wearing my carrot crown. I do a little twirl for him. Then Pa winks at me and says, "Sweet pea, you're the queen of the crop."

Chapter Two
Chicken Feather Tutus

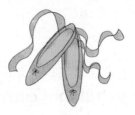

After a big lunch of fried chicken, potato salad, and thick slices of juicy red tomatoes, Lucy and I go outside to play.

Lucy begs, "Let's to go to the chicken house to hunt for eggs."

I say, "I'm not too sure. Those chickens are mean. They don't like it when you take their eggs, and I don't blame them!"

The hen house is behind the barn. I take my time getting there by asking Lucy lots of questions about the swan queen.

I ask, "What part do you want in the ballet?"

"I think I'd like to be a beautiful swan maiden," Lucy answers.

We walk around the farmhouse. Nanny's flowers are growing so pretty. I love the pink daisies best. Lucy likes the roses.

"Let's pick Nanny a bouquet of flowers for her kitchen window!" I suggest.

Lucy nods. "That's a great idea!" she says.

Picking flowers in a sunny spot makes me happy. The flowers spread across the bed like a rainbow. Rows of orange tiger lilies, yellow tulips, purple iris, my pink daisies, and Lucy's old fashioned red roses curve around the back of the house.

The bees are buzzing all over the honeysuckle vine.

"Do you think drinking from the honeysuckle vine helps the bees make more honey?" Lucy asks, grabbing up some tall white flowers.

"I don't know," I admit. "I can't remember what we learned about honey bees."

I put my face close to the blooms and take a deep breath. The flowers smell like heaven.

"Ooooh, smell your flowers!" I tell Lucy. "They smell delightful!

When we have enough flowers to fill a fruit jar, we take them to the back door and lay them on the steps. Through the big kitchen window, I can hear Nanny and Momma talking while they wash the lunch dishes.

I stand under the window and shout, "Nanny, we picked you some flowers!"

"Thank you, darlin'!" Nanny shouts back.

"Come on," Lucy says. "Let's get those eggs."

Even before we get to the chicken house, I can hear the hens going cluck, cluck, cluck. There's a big fence around the chicken house. From the gate, I see the little wooden boxes that make up the chicken house. Each hen has her own box full of sweet yellow straw.

Some of the boxes are empty. Those hens are not at home. If they are not on their nests, it's easier to get the eggs. We have to be sneaky to get past the ones who are home.

Lucy grabs the egg basket from the gatepost. Then she pushes the gate open, pulling me behind her. "Here we go!" she whispers. "Cluck like a chicken. Maybe we can fool them."

"Cluck, cluck-cluck, bawk, bawk," I cackle.

The chickens look pretty nervous as we walk across the pen. Their beady black eyes follow us. Lucy walks faster, so she's already to the chicken house when a circle of chickens starts gathering around me.

"I'm pretty sure we aren't fooling them," I say. "I'm trapped!"

The hens start to crowd around the chicken house steps, too. They want to see what Lucy is doing. I think they know that she's loading up her basket with their eggs. That's when I see a whole lot of white chicken feathers on the ground. An idea hits my brain like eggs on an iron skillet.

"Lucy, come quick! I got a plan," I shout. That makes the chickens run away.

Lucy turns around, smiling. She holds up her basket. It's full of eggs. "I've got twelve eggs in this basket. That's a bunch," she brags.

"Come on!" I say. I am picking up chicken feathers as fast as I can.

Lucy looks puzzled. "We came for eggs, not feathers," she says.

"I know, but these feathers will make two fine feather tutus just perfect for swan queens," I explain quickly, keeping my eyes on the chickens.

Lucy's eyes get big. She knows what I want to do! We gather up a whole pile of the feathers.

"I wish we had real tutus to glue them on," I say sadly.

"We could tuck them up under the sashes of our dresses," Lucy suggests.

I gasp. "That's the best idea you've had all day, Lucy!" I say. "Why didn't I think of that?"

Twirling, twirling, twirling, we dance around in our chicken feather tutus. We twirl till we fall over in a heap, giggling.

A shadow falls over us. It's T.J.

"Momma wants you," he says. Then he frowns. "What are you doing? Are you pretending to be that big bird that stands in front of the Chicken Bucket?" he asks, laughing.

"Can't you tell?" I say. T.J. can be so annoying. "We're beautiful swans!"

T.J. snorts. "Chickens are not the same as swans," he says. "Anyway, it's time to go. And Lil' Bit, if Momma sees those dirty feathers on your good dress, you're gonna be in big trouble!"

Chapter Three
The First Rule

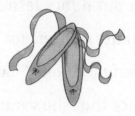

On Monday night, Lucy calls me on the phone. "Guess what?" she says.

I think for a second. "Did you get a new cat?" I ask.

"Nope," Lucy says. "Better."

"Did you find ten dollars?" I ask.

"Nope," Lucy says. "Better!"

"Did your momma win the lottery?" I ask.

Lucy laughs. "No, silly," she says. "Give up?"

"I give up!" I tell her.

"Tonight, after our dance lesson, Madame told us she needs so many dancers for the ballet that she is holding open auditions," Lucy tells me. I can hear from her voice that she's smiling.

My mouth drops open. "Are you joking?" I ask. "Is it true? Is Madame having open auditions? Can I try out to be in the ballet?"

"I knew you'd be excited!" she says. "Yes, it's true!"

After I hang up, I am so excited I can't believe it. "Ugly Brother! Ugly Brother!" I shout.

He pads sleepily past me and plops down on the floor next to my pink backpack.

I sit down beside him. "Guess what?" I say. "I'm going to audition for Swan Lake. Can't you just see me as the swan queen?"

He does not seem excited. In fact, he turns around, ignoring me.

"I don't like talking to your tail," I tell him. "What's wrong with you, Ugly Brother? Aren't you happy for me?"

Ugly Brother just whines. He must be sad about something. "Maybe a doggie treat will cheer you up," I say.

I get one from the kitchen, but he doesn't even lick it, so he must not be hungry.

It's cool in the house, so he's not too hot. Just from looking at him I can see that he probably just had a nap, so he can't be sleepy.

Finally, it hits me like rain in June.

"I know!" I shout. "You want to be a ballerina, too, just like me! Right, Ugly Brother? Is that what's wrong?"

Ugly Brother stands up and wags his tail. "Ruff ruff!" he barks. One bark means no. Two barks means yes!

"Okay," I tell him. "Don't worry. I'll teach you all the rules you need to know."

Ugly Brother barks twice. He's excited to learn all about being a ballerina. And I'm pretty excited to teach him!

Then I say, "Rule number one is a very important rule. Look at my feet." Then I point my toes. "Rule number one: Ballerinas always point their toes."

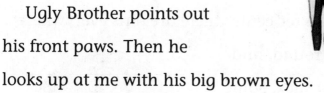

Ugly Brother points out his front paws. Then he looks up at me with his big brown eyes.

I pat him on the head. "Good job!" I say. "Now you're on your way to being a real true ballerina." And, I think to myself, I am one pirouette away from being the swan queen.

Chapter Four
Ballet Lessons

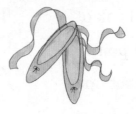

After school on Tuesday, Momma drives me
over to the rec center for my dance lesson. When
we get to the rec center there are girls everywhere;
short, tall, round, and
skinny as a stick. Some
girls are wearing T-shirts
and shorts, and some are
wearing leotards with tutus.
I have on my black shorts
and a pink princess shirt
with a sparkly silver crown.

I walk over and sit down on one of the wooden benches that line the room. Then I look around the dance studio.

It is really just a big bright room. Before it was the dance studio, it was a senior center, so they had to hang mirrors on one wall and put a long barre down the center of the room.

Little ballerinas are holding the barre as they plié, bending down low with their toes and knees pointed out. Some of the other girls are holding the barre as they practice standing on their toes. The older girls pirouette around the studio in their toe shoes.

Some of the older ballerinas have practiced a lot! They float through the air, light as a feather. Then they glide into their next move.

I watch them while I get my ballet shoes out of my bag. They are my cousin Lilly's old ballet slippers.

After I slide my feet into the slippers, I slowly and very carefully wind the long pink ribbons around my ankles, then tie the bows. I slip my bag under the bench, and then I am ready to go to the barre to take my place next to my friend Katie.

I make sure my feet are in the correct position as I bend low. In my head, I'm thinking *plié one, plié two, plié three.*

"Do you know about the auditions for Swan Lake?" Katie whispers.

"I sure do!" I whisper back. "Odette is the perfect part for me, since I'm going to be a queen."

Katie smiles. "I thought your cousin Lilly would get the part for Odette. I didn't know you'd try out too!" she says. When I nod, she says, "Good luck!"

"Shhh!" says our teacher, Ms. Dixie.

Ms. Dixie is tall like a tree. She is wearing a pink leotard and a long pink skirt and white toe shoes. The shoes are worn and scuffed.

As she moves around the room, she quietly talks to each girl. "You're a natural ballerina, Kylie Jean! Just look at your graceful arms," she tells me.

"Thank you," I say. "I always knew I was going to be a ballerina — and a beauty queen, of course."

Ms. Dixie just smiles and walks to the next girl.

When we're done warming up, Ms. Dixie calls, "Ballerinas gather around. I have an exciting announcement. Madame Girard wants you all to try out for a part in her recital of Swan Lake! The auditions are Saturday at nine a.m."

I know what part I want already! Odette is the lead role, so I will need to practice a lot of ballet moves. I decide I better ask for help. I raise my hand and ask, "Can you help me be Odette?"

Ms. Dixie claps her hands. "What a wonderful idea, Kylie Jean!" she exclaims. "We can all practice the dance steps. That way, everyone will be ready to try out!"

The other ballerinas all clap and cheer.

That's not what I meant at all! But I guess I don't care, as long as I get time to practice.

Chapter Five
School Surprise

The next morning, as soon as we get to our classroom, Cara, Lucy, and I start talking about the ballet. But when class starts, I can't stop thinking about being the Swan Queen.

Today Ms. Corazón tells our class she has a surprise for us. We beg her to tell us what it is, but she just smiles and says, "You will just have to wait until the end of the day."

At lunchtime, in the big, noisy cafeteria, Lucy, Paula, Cara, and I sit together. We try to guess what the surprise is.

"Maybe it's going to be free day on Friday," Cara says.

"Maybe we're going to get to go read to the kindergarten class," I say.

"Maybe we're getting a free homework pass," Lucy says.

"Maybe we're having a party!" Cara says.

Paula shakes her head. "I think you're all wrong. We'll just have to wait for our teacher to tell us," she says.

All afternoon, everyone's trying to figure out what the surprise is.

Finally, at the end of the day, Ms. Corazón passes out permission slips. She announces, "On Friday, the second grade is taking a field trip to see the ballet! We'll be seeing Cinderella. Isn't this exciting news, class?"

Before I can stop myself, I squeal! Queens are not squealers. Quickly, I cover my mouth with my hand.

I don't think anyone noticed. The girls are all too busy being excited. The boys don't seem too thrilled, though.

As for me, I can't wait. Watching the ballerinas might help me when I try out for the part of Odette. I can't believe how lucky I am!

"This is a dream come true! I can't wait to see the dancers," I say.

Lucy just keeps repeating, "I can hardly believe it. Pinch me!"

Paula finally does pinch her, but not too hard. She's just teasing.

Cara tells us, "One time my grandma took me to the ballet in the big city. The costumes the ballerinas wear are amazing! They have every color, with silk flowers sewn into their tutus. I think I'd want a blue one."

Lucy says, "I would love a purple tutu."

I bet you already know what color tutu I want.

That's right.

Pink!

When I get home, Momma is in the kitchen, rolling out biscuit dough.

I ask, "Momma, do you think you could sign my permission slip? It's to go to the ballet."

Momma signs her name in big, curly letters. When she hands the slip back to me, I put it right into my backpack. I don't want it to get lost!

Chapter Six
Seeing Cinderella

When we get off the bus in front of the ballet on Friday morning, I'm so excited that I feel like I could float away like a feather. Going to the ballet is a dream come true! Putting my hands over my head, I do a twirl on the sidewalk.

Lucy, Katie, and Cara are right next to me. On field trips we have the buddy system. I want to have Lucy for a buddy, but Cara gets Lucy and I get Katie.

The Performance Center is gigantic. It even has rows of seats upstairs. I hope we get to sit there!

A nice lady in a red jacket hands us each a program. That's a little book about the ballet.

Ms. Corazón tells us that we can use the program to follow the ballet and learn about the dancers.

I am disappointed when the lady in the red jacket leads us to our seats downstairs in the second row. At least we are close to the front.

Suddenly, we hear music coming from a big hole in front of the stage. Musicians sit there to play music for the ballerinas without distracting the folks watching them dance. I know I would rather watch the dancers!

The lights go down. Right away, it feels colder in the big room. Momma made me bring a sweater, so I put it on.

Then the curtains open, and I forget everything else.

Cara was right about the costumes. The stepsisters and the mean old stepmother are wearing the most beautiful costumes I've ever seen. But poor Cinderella! Her costume is an ugly brown dress without a tutu. Can you believe it?

The ballerinas float across the stage, telling the story of Cinderella through their dancing.

Cinderella dances with a broom, cleaning the house for her stepmother. I know that later she will get to dance with the prince. I watch carefully as the story goes on.

Then they suddenly stop dancing and the lights go up.

"What happened?" I ask. "What's going on? We didn't even get to see the prince yet!"

Ms. Corazón says, "Don't worry! The prince will come in the second act. This is a break they call intermission. You can use this time to read the program."

"Hey, guess what? It says in the program the part of Cinderella is performed by a prima ballerina!" Cara tells me. "Her name is Lizette Blanc."

"Oh, I sure hope we can meet her!" I say.

Soon, the lights turn off again. I look at Cinderella on the stage.

Her godmother helped her get ready for the ball. She looks real pretty with her dark hair up in a bun. Her white gown is long and she is wearing a sparkly tiara. Oooh, I just love tiaras! I hope Odette wears one.

The music starts. Right away, I'm lost in the fairy tale story. The ballroom scene is filled with so many costumes that I can't even see them all! Finally, the prince finds Cinderella.

The glass slipper fits her. Then they live happily ever after.

The ballet is over. The curtains go down and then they go right back up again. All of the dancers are on stage. They hold hands and bow.

My friends and I stand up and clap and clap. Even Cole and the other boys clap. Maybe they like ballet after all.

Then Ms. Corazón announces, "We are in for a treat! The prima ballerina, Lizette Blanc, is waiting to say hello to us." We all hurry, trying to move ahead, anxious to see her.

When we see her, Lizette Blanc looks as lovely as she did on stage, but now she is surrounded by school kids instead of princesses.

Soon it's my turn to talk to Lizette. I say, "Ever since I was an itty bitty baby I've wanted to be a queen, just like Cinderella. You found your prince and made your dream come true."

She smiles and asks, "Are you looking for a prince?"

"No, not really," I say. "But if I have to dance with one to wear a tiara, I will!" Then I tell her all about my plans to be Odette.

"Hurry up, Kylie Jean!" Lucy says. She is tapping me on the shoulder. I know she wants her turn, but Lizette is so nice! I hate to go.

Lucy steps up next to me.

"Miss Lizette, my turn is over, but this is my best cousin, Lucy," I say.

"You will be a wonderful Odette, little ballerina. Remember to point your toes!" Miss Lizette says.

"I will," I tell her. "I promise!"

Chapter Seven
Bubble Buns

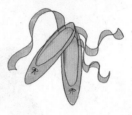

That night at supper I tell Momma, Daddy, T.J., and Ugly Brother all about the ballet.

"The Jacksonville Performance Center is better than the movie theater," I say.

Momma nods. "Your daddy and I saw a play there," she says. "It's very nice."

"I was shocked when Cinderella didn't have a tutu on her first costume," I go on. "But later she had on a long white gown and a sparkly tiara. It had so many tiny little diamonds. They looked like stars!"

Daddy says, "Sounds like you had a wonderful time, sugar."

"Yup, I sure did," I reply. Then I remember something else. "Miss Lizette Blanc, the prima ballerina, wears her hair in a bun. Momma, can you put my hair in a bun?"

Momma nods. Everyone at the table is finished, but I've been talking so much that I still have a lot of food on my plate.

"Maybe you should eat some supper now," Daddy suggests. "You can save some of this story for later."

Under the table, Ugly Brother barks twice. I guess he wants me to stop talking and eat, too.

"Okay, Daddy," I say. I start eating my veggies.

Between bites, I remind everyone that auditions for Swan Lake are tomorrow at nine o'clock. "Maybe I should go to bed right after I eat," I say, scooping up some peas.

"That's a little too early for bedtime. Why don't you help me with the dishes first?" Daddy says.

Daddy and I do the dishes. First I clear the table. Then I help him put the dishes into the dishwasher after he rinses them off. I like to put the spoons, forks, and knives in the little silverware baskets. I put all the spoons together so they can keep each other company. Then I do the same for the knives and forks, too.

When we're all done with the dishes, we watch TV. I only watch one show. Then Momma asks me, "Are you ready to take a bath now?"

"I sure am!" I say. I get up and head for the stairs.

Ugly Brother follows me. He likes to go with me when I take a bath. T.J. says Ugly Brother wants to drink the bathwater that spills on the floor, but I know it's because Ugly Brother really likes to bring me a towel. Sometimes he does lap up the bathwater a little bit, too.

"A bubble bath would be nice," I say. "What do you think, Ugly Brother?"

"Ruff, ruff," he barks. Two barks means yes!

I start to run the water. When it's nice and steamy, I pour in the bubble bath. But I put a little extra in by accident. It will be okay, since we like a lot of bubbles.

I get in the tub. Then I get a great idea. "Ugly Brother, I am going to give you the next rule for being a ballerina," I declare. "It is rule number two."

He gets real excited and jumps up on the edge of the tub. "Ruff, ruff!" he barks happily.

"Here it is, rule number two. Ballerinas have hair buns," I tell him. "I am going to have to get a hair bun tomorrow for my audition."

Then I pull my hair up in a pile on top of my head. "See? This is a bun," I say.

He whines and tries to stick his head under my pink towel. Oh no! This one will be hard for him, because he doesn't have much hair. Then an idea hits me like suds in a carwash.

"Come here," I say. Ugly Brother sits down right next to the tub. I pick up a big handful of bubbles and swirl them on top of his head.

"There you go, Ugly Brother!" I say. "You have your very own hair bun!"

He is so happy he chases his tail in a circle. Then he drags my pink towel over and holds it up to me. Bath time is over.

Later, with my head on my soft feather pillow, I drift off to sleep, thinking about being Queen of the Swans.

Chapter Eight
Dance Auditions

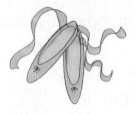

The next morning, I walk everywhere on my tiptoes. At the breakfast bar in the kitchen, I do a plié.

Momma says, "Honey, go wake up T.J. He has a game today and your daddy is waiting for him."

I tell her, "Okay, but I'm going to practice on my way, 'cause I have to be ready for tryouts."

I pirouette right before going up the stairs. I turn and do a plié on each step. On the first step, I say, "Plié one." On the next step, I say, "Plié two." On the third step, I say, "Plié three."

Momma yells, "Hurry up, Kylie Jean!"

I don't do any more pliés. I just run up the steps.

After I knock on T.J.'s door, I do a perfect arabesque, stretching my arm out and my leg behind me with carefully pointed toes.

"T.J.!" I yell. "Momma says you're gonna be late for the soccer tournament, so wake up!"

Two seconds later, he almost knocks me over as he runs out of his room. "What time is it?" he asks.

From downstairs, Daddy shouts, "Hurry up, son! It's eight o'clock! I'll be waiting in the car."

My tummy is rumbling, so I go downstairs and start eating breakfast while T.J. gets ready.

When he runs down the stairs, I say, "Good luck! I hope your team wins." He smiles, gives me a high five, and dashes out the door. Then it's just Momma and me.

I'm getting so nervous! It feels like I have a stomach full of June bugs.

Momma brushes my shiny brown hair and puts it up in a bun. Then I get dressed. I'm wearing my black shorts and my pink t-shirt with the princess crown on the front for good luck. I have my ballet slippers tucked into my bag.

Finally, it's time to go!

Madame Girard's dance studio is in an old house. The bottom floor is where the dance lessons are. Madame lives upstairs. In the studio, the walls are all painted a pink as soft as rose petals.

The room is full of dancers. All of Madame's girls are wearing black leotards and pink tutus. I can tell that most of the girls who take classes with Ms. Dixie, like I do, are wearing shorts.

The older girls are warming up at the barre. I see my cousin Lilly there. She looks beautiful! Littler girls are doing pliés and stretching. I look around the room for Lucy. I'm as nervous as a cat in a bathtub.

"You'll be awesome," Momma tells me. "Just dance your best." Then she gives me a little push forward, and I go to stretch with the younger girls.

Madame watches with a clipboard from the corner of the room. She is tiny and dressed all in black. Her black hair is in a ballerina bun and her black eyes don't miss anything.

Once we are all done stretching, Madame says, "You will each announce the part you are trying out for. Then you will dance."

The older girls dance first. My cousin Lilly takes my breath away! She flits across the room like she has butterfly wings. When she dances it is just like seeing Lizette Blanc.

When it is time for the younger girls we all warm up at the barre together.

Then Madame calls my name.

As I take the floor, I softly say, "I am dancing the part of Odette."

Madame frowns a little when she hears me. Lilly winks at me.

Counting my steps quietly under my breath, I begin.

Then suddenly there is nothing but the dance. It seems like I just started when I end with a jump followed by an arabesque.

No one claps or cheers. I know that Madame would not allow it. It's so quiet you could hear the feathers on hummingbird wings.

Momma is smiling at me. Madame smiles too, just a little, and marks something on her clipboard.

After everyone dances, Madame announces, "I will post the parts for the ballet on Monday."

I whisper, "That seems like one hundred days from now. How can I wait until Monday?"

Katie groans. "I don't know," she says. "It's a long, long time to wait."

I grab my bag and follow Momma out to the van. We head home.

Momma says, "Time will pass faster than you think."

I sure hope she's right.

Chapter Nine

Not Odette

On Monday right after school, I ride my bike all the way over to Madame's dance studio. I speed down Peachtree Street with my pink handlebar streamers blowing in the wind. Ugly Brother has to run to follow me. He can hardly keep up.

When we get to Madame's studio, I hop off my bike and sprint to the door. A creamy piece of paper is tacked to it.

In curly black writing are the names of all of the ballerinas, and next to them are the parts in the ballet.

I look for my name, but the first name on the list is Lilly. She will be playing Odette.

My heart sinks way down to my toes.

It says "swan maiden" next to my name. Katie, Lucy, and Cara are all swan maidens too.

"Ugly Brother, I'm not the swan queen," I say sadly. "I'm just a swan maiden. I can't believe it. I didn't get to be Odette."

Ugly Brother just whines and puts his paws over his face. Crying a little, I sit down on the porch steps. Ugly Brother comes over to lick my face. He can tell I'm as sad as a dog who's lost his bone.

"We can't cry all day, Ugly Brother," I say, wiping my face with my shirt. "I'm happy for Lilly. She should be Odette."

Then I think of something. "Maybe this is a good time to tell you the next rule for being a ballerina!"

"Ruff, ruff!" says Ugly Brother.

"Rule number three is: Ballerinas are always graceful. It's okay to get a smaller part if a better ballerina gets the big one," I explain. "You just have to be graceful. When I get home, I'll call Lilly and tell her congratulations. She earned the part of the queen. Now I'll show you how to dance gracefully," I add. "Just watch me!"

He barks, "Ruff, ruff."

I do a perfect arabesque. Ugly Brother tries to do a turn, but he just looks like he's chasing his tail! He is not a graceful dancer, but at least he knows the main rules for being a ballerina.

Besides, he acts graceful lots of times by being nice. I pat him on the head and say, "Good job, Ugly Brother!"

Seems to me you can be a chicken one day and feathers the next or a dog one day and a ballerina the next.

Chapter Ten

Practice Makes Perfect

For the next two weeks, I will have ballet practice two times a week! I have to go to classes with Ms. Dixie and with Madame.

Ballet practice with Madame is on Thursday and Friday. When I arrive at the dance studio, the only people there are the other girls performing in Swan Lake. My cousins Lilly and Lucy smile at me and Lilly gives a little wave.

Madame begins to give us drills to do. These are just dance steps that we repeat a bunch of times. She counts in French. "Un, deux, trois."

She has a long black stick, and she taps it on the floor as she counts. The tapping of the stick makes it hard to concentrate, and my feet get all tangled up. I made a mistake. My feet are in the wrong position.

Madame sees them with her dark bird-like eyes. Madame sees everything all the time.

The tapping stick stops. Madame asks the ballerinas to sit. She adds coldly, "Everyone except Kylie Jean, *s'il vous plait*." When I frown, she says, "That means 'please.'" Then she makes me repeat the dance step over and over.

Madame says, " Again, again, again!" She points to my legs and feet with the black stick. My feet find the right position. Carefully, I repeat it again and again.

I am so embarrassed, even when Madame finally says, "*Tres bien.*" That means very good, but I just feel bad.

When I finally get to join the younger girls on the bench, I whisper, "I wish I was back in Ms. Dixie's class!"

Katie says, "I know. Me too!"

I think to myself that it can't be worth it to keep coming for lessons if Madame gets so mad when I make a little mistake.

Then I remember something. I'm doing all of this to be a swan maiden. I wished I could be in Swan Lake.

Getting my wish means I have to try to be the best swan maiden ever.

For the rest of our lesson, I listen to everything Madame says. My eyes are on her and on Lilly at all times. You can learn a lot just by watching.

By the end of our lesson, I can tell I'm getting better! My feet know the steps, even when I feel nervous.

Lucy whispers, "You're looking like a real true swan maiden, Kylie Jean."

Momma walks into the studio to pick me up. I run through the dance steps one more time.

Watching me dance, Momma's face lights up like a firefly.

When Madame nods her head, signaling that I can go, I grab my ballet bag.

Outside on the porch, Momma gives me a big old squeezy hug. She whispers, "You are a beautiful little ballerina. I am so proud of you!"

"Thanks, Momma," I say, smiling. "At first, it was really hard, and I made a mistake."

"But you kept trying, right?" Momma asks. I nod, and she says, "That's the part that proves you're a real ballerina."

Chapter Eleven
A Prince for Odette

When we get to Madame's studio on Friday, there are ballerinas waiting on her porch. It seems like everyone is outside.

"Where is Madame?" I ask Momma.

Momma shrugs. "She didn't call to cancel your lesson," she says, "so I guess she's just running late."

We weave our way up the steps through groups of tutus. Lilly and Lucy make their way toward us.

"Hey, Kylie Jean. Hi, Aunt Shelly," Lucy says.

Lilly smiles and takes my hand. "Don't worry," she tells Momma. "I'll look after Kylie Jean."

Momma says, "Aren't you sweet, Lilly! Thank you for keeping an eye on her. I'm going to run over to the Piggly Wiggly. I'll be back after class." Momma leaves. Then Lilly and Lucy and I sit down and chat for a while.

When Madame arrives a few minutes later, she seems strange. Her hair is messy and she isn't wearing her ballet slippers like she always does.

We start practicing, and she holds the clipboard, but she doesn't notice any mistakes because she is staring into space. Several times, she loses count with the black stick. Her tapping sounds more like rain than rhythm.

What's wrong with Madame? She doesn't even notice the hum of the ballerinas whispering. I wonder if Madame is sick.

Finally, I can't stand it anymore. I have to know what's going on, so I go to right up to her. Madame doesn't see me at first, but Lilly does. Lilly waves at me to come back to the barre. Shaking my head, I wait. It takes a while, but finally, Madame sees me.

"Yes, Kylie Jean, what is it?" she asks.

"Are you okay, Madame?" I ask quietly.

I am shocked when Madame crumples. She sits down on the bench. She doesn't cry, but she looks like she wants to. She even covers her face with her hands. The dancers have stopped dancing. They start walking over.

"My beautiful dancers, there is a big problem!" Madame confesses. "The boy who was going to be the prince has broken his ankle. He may never dance again. It is so sad."

I gasp. Everyone begins to whisper. One little ballerina starts to cry.

We have worked so hard! I kind of want to cry too, but beauty queens are never quitters.

"Our ballet is ruined!" Madame says. "We can't perform Swan Lake without a prince for Odette."

One girl asks, "Can another girl dance the role of the prince?"

Madame shakes her head and explains, "The prince must lift Odette many, many times. None of you are strong enough to be the prince."

We all think some more, but no one has any good ideas. Finally, Madame claps her hands. "We are done for today," she says. "Class is dismissed. I have to think!"

Momma is not here to pick me up yet, so Lilly, Lucy, and I sit on the porch waiting for her. We are all too sad to talk much. This is Lilly's big chance to be the prima ballerina, and my first chance to be a swan maiden. I don't want it to be ruined.

Lilly tries to cheer us up. She says, "Madame will figure it out. Don't worry."

"I wish that boy didn't break his ankle," Lucy says.

I nod and say, "Me too, but we can't change it, so we have to find a new prince. Right?"

When Momma pulls up, I wave goodbye to my cousins. "Don't worry, Lilly," I say. "I'm gonna think of a plan so you get to be Odette."

All the way home, I think about boys I know. I have lots of friends who are boys, but none of them seem like ballerinas.

At home, after I help Momma bring in the groceries, I get a purple Popsicle from one of the bags. Ugly Brother and I have the Popsicle on the back steps. I have a lick and then he has one. I like sharing Popsicles with Ugly Brother.

I tell Ugly Brother all about our ballet boy troubles. He whines a little, but I'm not sure if he feels bad for us or if he just wants more of the Popsicle.

"You want another lick?" I ask, holding out the frozen treat.

He barks excitedly, "Ruff, ruff." Then he bites the end off.

"Popsicles are for licking!" I say.

But I can't be mad at Ugly Brother. He just likes purple Popsicles, and so do I.

Then T.J. walks up. When he sees all the purple sweetness on my face and on Ugly Brother's, he laughs. "You've got doggie germs now," he teases me. "You're probably gonna grow a tail."

When I look up at T.J., an idea hits my brain like syrup on a snow cone. I whisper to Ugly Brother, "Are you thinking what I'm thinking?"

"Ruff, ruff!" he barks.

You just know I have a plan to get a prince for Odette! I tell T.J. all about our ballerina problem and how sad Lilly is. Lilly is one of his favorite cousins. He seems real sorry, but doesn't offer to help.

I take a deep breath. This isn't easy. Then I say, "You could be the prince. None of your friends would ever see you dancin', because they don't go to the ballet anyway. It would make all the ballerinas so happy, especially Lilly."

"I'm not a dancer," he says.

"You wouldn't have to do much dancing," I say.

He frowns, but I can tell he's thinking about it. "What would I have to do?" he asks.

"You would be lifting Lilly while she dances," I explain. "And since you're real strong I know you can do it for sure."

T.J. hesitates. "I don't know," he says. "I'm not a dancer." He thinks for a long, long time. At first I think he's going to say no. Then he takes a deep breath and says, "Let's make a deal. Will you promise to clean my room for a whole month?"

I snort. "Some deal!" I mutter. "I'd rather clean out Granny's cat box for a month!"

But what can I do? We have to have a prince.

So I stick out my hand and say, "We better shake on it."

Chapter Twelve
A Princess After All

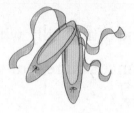

T.J. comes with me to Madame Girard's studio next time we have practice. He looks funny, standing there in his gray sweat pants with ballerinas all around him. He's usually on the soccer field surrounded by big, sweaty soccer players. Lilly looks shocked to see him!

I take T.J.'s hand and pull him over to Madame.

"Who is this?" she asks, frowning.

"This is the new prince!" I tell her. "My very own brother, T.J. Carter, is going to be a ballerina. But we can't tell anyone! Okay?"

T.J. turns as red as a robin's belly and shuffles his feet.

Madame gushes, "I am so thrilled!"

"I still have to make time for soccer practice," T.J. says. "I'm just doing this dancing thing to help out my sister and my cousin Lilly."

"I promise to work around your soccer schedule for your lessons," Madame says.

T.J. and Lilly already know each other, so they'll be good partners. Lilly squeals and gives T.J. a big hug when she finds out he'll be the prince.

Madame tells me, "Your brother is perfect. He is an athlete, so he will have no trouble lifting Lilly."

During practice, Madame spends all of her time working with T.J. and Lilly.

T.J. is a quick learner, and luckily he doesn't have to do much. Mostly, he is just there for the lifts.

Lucy, Cara, Katie, and I are practicing too. Our big part is dancing around Odette when she is changing from a swan to a girl. We have to make a little half circle around her.

Since Lilly is busy practicing with T.J., we pretend that a stool is Odette. We all move forward together, reaching out our arms like fluttering wings.

Gathering around the stool, we wait for Odette and the prince to dance together.

Finally, when they do, we swan maidens leap joyfully in the background.

When we are done with the rehearsal, Madame claps her hands. Her eyes sparkle, and she says, "Kylie Jean, getting your brother to be the prince is a real feather in your cap! You saved our ballet!"

Everyone begins to take off their ballet slippers and pack up their bags. Lucy and I sit side by side, best ballerina buddies and best cousins.

T.J. is talking to Lilly about their dance. They are best cousins too. It is nice to have such a big family. When someone needs help, all we have to do is ask and usually someone figures out how to help, just like T.J. and me.

Madame calls out, "We only have one practice session left, tomorrow afternoon. On Saturday morning at nine o'clock, we'll have a dress rehearsal at the high school. I will see you then, dancers. *Au revoir.* Goodbye!"

I can't wait to see my costume. It will be all white because I'm a swan maiden. And I bet it'll be a lot better than chicken feathers. I lean over to Lucy and whisper, "No more farm tutus for us!"

I am very excited. If T.J. is a prince, then that makes me a princess!

Chapter Thirteen

Dress Rehearsal

Early next Saturday morning, Momma makes pancakes that are light as a feather. She mixes them in a big blue bowl and I get to pour the milk in. Then we make giant pancakes as big as a plate on our old black griddle.

I'm standing on my stepstool, reaching for the syrup, when T.J. walks into the kitchen.

He laughs. Then he reaches over my head, saying, "I've got this one, shorty!"

T.J. puts the maple syrup on the table. Then he pulls out a chair and sits down. Daddy walks in, too.

"I helped make the pancakes," I announce.

"They look delicious!" Daddy says.

He puts the plate of pancakes on the table. Then Momma brings a plate piled high with crispy bacon. We all start eating.

Pretty soon, we hear Ugly Brother begging for some bacon. Momma gives me a stern look because she knows I want to feed him under the table.

Daddy asks, "T.J., what will your friends on the football team have to say about you being in the ballet?"

"I don't know," T.J. says. "But it's a lot harder than it looks. I've only been to a couple of lessons, and I have to be ready for the performance. I don't want to let Madame, Lilly, and Kylie Jean down."

Momma checks her watch. Then she says, "You two better hurry and eat your breakfast or you'll be late for rehearsal!"

Soon, the empty plates are stacked in the kitchen sink. T.J. will drive us to the high school.

When we get there, he lets me out in front of the doors and then goes to park his truck.

We will rehearse and perform in the high school auditorium. It's nice, but not as nice as the Jacksonville Performance Center where we went to see Cinderella.

As I'm going up to the front door, I turn to look for T.J., but he's nowhere to be seen! I don't even spot his truck in the parking lot. I see girls rushing all over the place, but I don't see my brother.

Lucy runs up to me, holding out her extra tutu and leotard. I am borrowing them for the ballet. "I can't find my brother," I tell Lucy.

She doesn't look worried. "He probably went to park somewhere else," she says. "So his friends won't know he's here if they happen to drive by."

I smack my forehead. "Of course!" I say. "Oh, Lucy, you have set my mind at ease." Then Lucy and I head inside the school.

All of the swan maidens are wearing beautiful headbands with white feathers and leotards and fluffy tutus.

You won't believe it, but makeup is part of our costume too! I never get to wear makeup. The older ballerinas help us put it on in the dressing room. The dressing room is really one of the locker rooms, but we can pretend we are backstage at a big, fancy theater.

Lilly puts white powder all over my face. The she adds some pink to my cheeks and lips. She tells me, "Keep your hands off of your face, or you'll mess up my excellent makeup job. Okay? And be careful to not get any water on your face, either."

I gasp when I see my face in the mirror. "I look so pretty!" I whisper. "I want to look like this forever. I'll never take a bath again!"

Lilly laughs. "You can always put on more makeup later, and baths are important," she tells me. "Especially bubble baths."

I have to remember to share this new rule with Ugly Brother! Rule number four: Ballerinas get to wear beautiful makeup. Ugly Brother can wear lipstick if he doesn't try to eat it first.

I leave the locker room and see T.J. walking down the hall.

He's wearing tights, pants that go to his knees, a white ruffled shirt, and a sky-blue vest. His face is white as a clean cotton sheet.

Lilly comes out and stands next to him. She looks so beautiful that when I see her I forget she's my cousin. She looks like a real, true queen!

We all go into the auditorium. Tapping her black stick on the stage, Madame calls out, "Places, everyone! We are ready to begin our ballet."

I do not make one mistake during the whole entire dress rehearsal. Not even a little tiny one. T.J. has to repeat his entrance twice, but his lifts are awesome.

After we're all done, Madame tells us that we are ready for our big day. Clapping her hands, she exclaims, "The performance will be wonderful, *magnifique!*"

Chapter Fourteen
Swan Lake

That night, right before the performance, Lilly looks calm and beautiful. She really is a prima ballerina. But Madame Girard is as nervous as a cat in a car.

She keeps checking on things. First she checks on the music. Then she checks with the set crew. After that she talks to all the ballerinas and T.J., too.

Everyone gets a final check from Madame Girard. She checks to make sure our makeup is perfect and that our tutus have no rips.

She looks at me first. Then, while she checks Cara, Lucy, and Katie, I peek through the curtain.

There are a ton of people here! I see Momma, Daddy, Nanny, Pa, Granny, and Pappy. Plus all of my aunts and uncles and cousins and friends.

It is so exciting to dance for all the people I love to the moon and back! I wish Ugly Brother could see me dance too, but dogs are not allowed at the ballet.

All of us swan maidens sit down on a bench backstage, waiting. We smile and swing our legs, swaying together in our fluffy tutus.

I thought I would be nervous, but I'm having too much fun to get butterflies in my tummy. Sometimes it is better to not be the queen! Can you believe I said that?

Then Ms. Dixie comes back to check on all of her ballerinas. "Y'all are going to be amazing swan maidens!" she exclaims.

Then she gives each of us a big squeezy hug. When she hugs me, she whispers, "You make me proud out there, you hear?"

Just then Madame Girard says, "*Vite, vite!*" That means hurry up fast in French.

It is time for the ballet to begin.

As we line up to go onto the stage, Madame reminds us, "Ballerinas, be sure to point your toes! And reach your arms all the way to the tips of your fingers!"

"Don't worry," I tell her. "We'll be perfect swan maidens."

The swan maidens gather in a circle around Lilly. Then we sail across the stage, telling our story.

Our white feathers fan out as we float through the air like flying birds. When we are girls we glide gently across the stage.

I see Pa wink at me in the audience, but I have to be a swan maiden right now, so I can't wink back. Then we slowly move to the back of the stage.

Odette is alone. She is sad and then T.J. — I mean the prince — comes. They dance together, and you can see their joy.

The prince lifts Odette, twirling her around. T.J. looks so handsome and doesn't even mess up, not once.

I can't believe it! T.J. might just be a dancer after all!

Suddenly, they leap gracefully across the stage and duck through the curtain.

Odette and her prince have flown away to escape the evil spell.

Now it's our turn to dance. The swan maidens leap with joy as the curtain goes down.

Then it goes up again, and we all stand on the stage, holding hands, to take a bow. T.J. is holding my hand.

I see Uncle Bay smiling and clapping for me. Momma blows me kisses. Mr. Jim is waving. Daddy is shouting, "Bravo."

T.J. gives my hand a little squeeze.

Then he bends down and whispers in my ear, "You know, Kylie Jean, a swan maiden can grow up to be a queen."

I want to give him a big ole hug, but he wouldn't like it in front of all of these people. I'll save that hug for Ugly Brother later.

I blow kisses to all my fans in the front row. They deserve some sugar for coming to our ballet. Then, just as the curtain starts to go down, I can't resist. I give a little beauty queen wave, nice and slow, side to side.

I'm pretty sure that T.J. is right. I am going to grow up to be a queen.

Kylie Jean

Spelling Queen

Table of Contents

Chapter One
Easy as Pie

Mondays are spelling test days. So every Sunday night right before I go to bed, I have to practice my spelling words. Today is Sunday. I'm ready to go!

First, I get my spelling words list. Then I write all of the words five times each. Using a piece of notebook paper and a pink pencil, I write, "Pie, pie, pie, pie, pie." (Before I learned this trick, I wasn't a very good speller.)

When I finish writing down all the words, I decide to go to the kitchen for some of Momma's tasty apple pie. A is for apple. When I turn on the kitchen light, Ugly Brother is standing right in the middle of the room, waiting for some pie.

"Are you hungry for pie too?" I ask him.

He turns his head to the side and barks, "Ruff, ruff."

Two barks means yes. This does not surprise me one teeny tiny bit, since Ugly Brother is always hungry. I carefully scoot the pie plate off of the counter and onto the table. Then I scoop out a big messy piece of pie.

Plop! It lands in the middle of the paper plate. Then an idea hits my brain like cinnamon on toast!

Holding the plate, I suggest, "How about I get some pie for you and you help me study my words?"

Ugly Brother is already licking his lips. He barks, "Ruff, ruff."

I say, "We have a deal!" I put his plate on the floor and cut another piece of pie for myself. Ugly Brother eats his pie in two giant bites. Gobble! Gobble! Then he licks his plate.

When I'm done eating, Ugly Brother helps me with my spelling. I explain, "I'll spell the word. Then you bark two times if I'm right and one time if I'm wrong."

I put the list on the floor where he can see it. Then I start to spell. The words are: all, does, hid, people, find, sheep, book, train, jar, and pie.

The first three words are easy as pie, but then I have to spell people.

I spell, "P-e-e-p-l-e," and Ugly Brother barks, "RUFF!"

"You know what, I can spell that word," I say. "But that sneaky o gets me every time."

"What are you talking about?" T.J. asks as he walks into the room.

"Just a tricky spelling word," I reply.

T.J. puts half of the pie on his plate and pulls a fork from the kitchen drawer. He pours a big glass of milk to go with it.

"Are you trying to spell delicious?" he asks. "Because this pie is delicious!" He shovels the pie into his mouth.

"Momma would say you have bad manners," I tell him. "Even if you do think her pie is good."

T.J. ignores me. He asks, "Do you want me to help you study?"

Ugly Brother barks, "Ruff!"

That means no thank you. Picking up my spelling list, I head for the door. "No thanks," I reply. "I have Ugly Brother helping me."

Between bites, T.J. mumbles, "Suit yourself, Lil' Bit. You do know he's a dog, right?"

Clenching my teeth, I hiss, "Shhh. He thinks he's a real true person!"

Ugly Brother is already climbing the steps when I catch up with him. We study my words some more.

After a while, Daddy comes to tuck us in. He peeks around the corner and tells me, "Bedtime, princess."

Daddy kisses me on both of my cheeks and pulls the covers up to my nose, then kisses Ugly Brother on the tip top of his head.

As he turns out the light, I whisper, "I love you to the moon and back."

Daddy smiles and says, "I love you a bushel and a peck." He leaves the door open a crack, so the hall light can make a tiny glowing path across my bedroom floor. Then he tiptoes back downstairs.

Chapter Two
Super Spellers

The next day when I get to school, I sit down at my usual table with my best cousin, Lucy, and our friends Cara and Paula.

Paula seems really worried. She is very quiet, and Miss Paula Dupree is never quiet.

"Did you study for the test?" I ask.

She moans. "I forgot to learn the new words!" she whispers.

"Oh, no!" Lucy says.

"Don't worry," I say. "We'll help you with your spelling when we go to recess. Right, girls?"

Lucy and Cara are both super good spellers!

"Sure will," Lucy agrees.

"I know them all," Cara chimes in.

Paula sighs. "I sure hope y'all can help me learn the words extra fast," she says.

We all nod in agreement just as Ms. Corazón starts our morning math lesson. Math takes a long, long time. About fifty hours! Well, it seems that long, anyway.

I whisper, "Is that clock stuck? It's moving as slow as a possum at noon."

Lucy shakes her head. "No, it's right," she says. "We're the ones that are slow."

We do our practice problems. Finally, it's time for morning recess. Yay! We dash out the door, heading for the swings. Today we're lucky because there are four of us girls and four empty swings. Cole and the boys try to race for the swings, but we get there first. B is for boy.

Lucy has the spelling word list.

"I know all the words by heart," I announce, swinging high.

Lucy swishes past me. "Oh, good," she says. "I'll call them out, Paula can spell them, and you can check to see if she's right."

Cara asks, "What about me?"

I think for a second. Then I say, "You can remember the ones she misses."

We swing and spell.

Lucy swings out, calling, "All."

Paula says, "That's an easy one. A-L-L."

I swing in, shouting, "Ta-da! You're right!"

Every time Paula gets one right, we all cheer. Ta-da!

We keep on like that: swing in, spell, swing out, ta-da! It's a pattern, just like in math today.

"Don't forget the bonus word," I tell Paula. "If you miss a word, it can help you still make a hundred on your test!"

Paula says, "You are all the best friends ever. With your help, I think I'm going to make an A on this spelling test." She leaps off the swing and lands on her feet on the ground.

Back in the classroom, Ms. Corazón tells us to get out our paper and pencils. It is time for the spelling test.

Paula looks nervous, so I lean across our desks.

"Now, don't you worry," I tell her. "Just remember spelling on the playground. Swing, spell, ta-da! This test is gonna be as easy as p-i-e."

Paula nods. "I know, and pie is one of our words!" she says.

I whisper, "I know," and we all give Paula a thumbs up.

Ms. Corazón is ready. She will call out the spelling word, say it in a sentence, and then repeat it. We have ten spelling words. The word "ten" was on last week's list! Ms. Corazón says, "Sheep. Sheep live on the farm. Sheep."

I giggle. This is so funny, because Pa's Lickskillet Farm doesn't even have any sheep!

She keeps reading the words. I am pretty sure I spell them all right.

The bonus word is "letter." I know that one!

When the test is over, we each grade our own paper. I got every single one right!

Ms. Corazón asks, "Who made a hundred on their test?"

We all raise our hands, even Paula. That makes us all super spellers. Then I say, "I got the bonus word right, too. Ta-da!"

Lucy, Cara, and Paula chime in, "Ta-da!"

Chapter Three
The Cutest Cat

That afternoon, Lucy rides home on the bus with me. Usually her momma picks her up, but today she's getting her hair done at the Kut and Kurl beauty shop.

We hop up three steps to get on the bus.

Lucy says, "1, 2, 3."

I say, "A, B, C."

My favorite bus driver, Mr. Jim, puts his hand up. "Whoa," he says, and we stop.

He asks, "Does your cousin have a note from her momma to ride the bus?"

"Yes sir," Lucy says. She hands him the note and we go find a seat.

The girl behind us is writing a letter for her homework. Her name is Emily. She asks, "Hey, how do you spell 'dear'?"

I think about it. "Is it deer like the animal or dear like, Dear Lucy?"

"Not the animal one," Emily says, smiling.

Lucy says, "That's easy. D-E-A-R."

Lucy and I play tic-tac-toe on notebook paper. The bus gets louder and louder as more kids get on it. But once we start dropping kids off, the bus gets quieter and quieter.

When we get to Peachtree Lane, we hop down the steps to get off the bus.

Lucy says, "A, B, C."

I say, "1, 2, 3."

As we walk up the sidewalk, Lucy asks, "What do you want to do till my momma comes to get me?"

I'm thinking about her question. But then I hear something coming from the bushes right by the front door. "Meow, meeooow." I look at Lucy and Lucy looks at me!

She asks, "Did you get a cat?"

"No, not yet, but maybe I'm getting one today!" I say. I throw down my backpack and circle the hedge, calling, "Here, kitty, kitty. Come on out. I want to be your friend."

Lucy watches me. She's not sure about a strange cat that we don't even know yet. She frowns and says, "Maybe we should go get your momma."

Just then I see part of the cat under the bush. "No," I whisper. "It's a beautiful little cat. I'm sure it's very nice, so would you please help me catch it, Lucy?"

We both get down on our knees in the grass, peering under the bushes. Suddenly we see the cat. I squeal. It's a cute little kitten! It's a tiny white ball of fur, with a sweet face, a little pink nose, and a black patch over one eye.

Lucy leans back. "I wonder where the momma cat is," she says.

I throw myself down on the ground, and then crawl like a spider right up under that bush and rescue the poor baby cat. Then I carefully inch my way back out, holding the little kitten close to keep it safe.

Lucy is shocked! The number one beauty queen rule is to not get dirty, and I am covered with dirt like a monster truck at the mud bowl.

I hand the kitten to Lucy so I can dust myself off. Once my clothes aren't dirty anymore, I reach out and say, "Give it back now."

Lucy shakes her head. She says, "I'm going to be this kitten's momma."

Now I'm shocked! After I went to all the trouble to get that kitten, Lucy is trying to be its momma instead of me.

I think fast. "Lucy, I love you, and you are my best cousin," I begin. "But I just saved that cat, so I am the momma."

Lucy starts to cry. I feel bad. Too bad we didn't find two kittens. Then an idea hits my brain like summer catfish in a hot skillet. Since we only have one, we'll have to share it!

I put my arm around Lucy's shoulder. "I have an idea," I tell her. "We can both be the kitten's momma!"

She sniffs. Then she asks, "Where will our baby cat live?"

I think about it for a minute.

"Well, sometimes the kitty can live in the country with you," I say. "And sometimes it can live in town with me."

Lucy is cheering up, and she hands the kitten to me. Just then, Momma comes out and cries, "Where on earth did you get that cat?"

"I found it in our yard in the bushes because it wants to live with me, and Lucy too sometimes," I say. "Please let us keep it, Momma. This baby kitten needs us!"

Lucy adds, "Please, Aunt Shelly!"

Momma takes the cat and looks it over real good. "This is a girl kitty," she says. Then she asks, "Does she have a name?"

Lucy and I look at each other.

I say, "Princess."

She says, "Patches."

Momma looks at Lucy. "You'll have to do some fast talkin' to get your momma to let you have a cat," Momma says. "She doesn't even like cats."

Lucy frowns. "I know my momma will love Patches," she says. "Please?"

"I'm still not convinced we need a cat," Momma says. "What about Ugly Brother?"

"Well, he would like a little sister," I tell her. "I just know it."

Momma thinks for a while. I hop from one foot to the other, over and over. Finally, Momma says, "You can keep the kitty if Lucy's momma says it's okay, if you promise to look after it, and if Ugly Brother can get used to having a cat around."

Lucy and I squeal and hug each other. Then we hug Momma.

"Thank you, Momma!" I say.

Momma smiles and hands the kitty to us.

"Can we please please please name her Patches?" Lucy asks me. "Pretty please?"

"Okay," I say. "If we can put a pink collar on her."

Lucy smiles and nods. "That'll be fine," she says. "Just fine!"

Chapter Four
Be in the Bee?

As soon as we get to school on Tuesday, Lucy and I tell everyone about Patches. When we see Cara and Paula we shout excitedly, "We have a kitten!"

Cara smiles. "Two new kittens? How fun!" she says. "They're going to be best friends."

I shake my head. "Just one kitten," I explain. "We're going to share her."

"What's her name?" Paula asks.

"It's Patches," Lucy tells her. "I picked it out. Isn't it the cutest name ever?"

"Princess would have been better," I say. "She is the cutest little white cat with a black patch over one eye. That's why Lucy decided her name should be Patches."

"Take your seats, class," Ms. Corazón says. "I have an important announcement!"

I am not sure what could be more important than a new kitty, but I go straight to my seat anyway. Beauty queens are not rule breakers, and they always follow directions.

Ms. Corazón explains, "Next Monday, we will be having a class spelling bee. The winner will get a blue ribbon and then be in the school-wide spelling bee."

The whole class hums with excitement as our teacher passes out a practice list of words. This is exciting because I am a fantastic speller now. But it's not exciting because practicing for the spelling bee will be a lot of work.

When we go to the cafeteria for lunch, Paula is pushing peas around on her lunch tray because peas are not her favorite. Today they have fried chicken, peas, salad, and a roll. I brought my lunch in my pink lunchbox. It has lots of pretty little hearts all over it.

I say, "Y'all, help me think. Should I be in the bee? What's good about the spelling contest? What's bad? Is it the kind of thing a beauty queen should do?"

Lucy points out, "There isn't really a spelling bee queen, so there's no crown."

Cara says, "I think it's good practice for talking in front of a lot of people. Beauty queens have to be good talkers."

Paula adds, "Even if you don't get to wear a crown, it's probably okay to wear your best pink dress. You would get a blue ribbon if you win."

I take out my thermos. Then I pour my tomato soup with ABCs into a little bowl. As I stir, a Y pops up, then an E, and a S.

I can't believe it, but there is a word in my bowl! I shout, "My soup says yes! Besides, everyone knows beauty queens have to be smart too, so I just have to be in the bee!"

Together we look at the list of words to study. Some words are so hard, like "orange," and some are so easy, like "six."

Paula says, "You might need help with the hard words. We'll all help you study, just like you helped me!"

I wink at my friends. They're the best friends in the whole wide world! "I knew I could count on y'all," I tell them.

The big yellow lunchroom is noisy, but we start to practice anyway. They call the words and I try to spell them. Lucy puts a star next to the ones I still need to study some more.

I can't wait to tell Momma, Daddy, T.J., Ugly Brother, and Patches all about the big spelling bee!

That night at the dinner table, I tell everyone my news. Except Patches. I can't tell her because she's not home. I keep forgetting that she lives at Lucy's house sometimes.

I say, "Today, our teacher told us that we're going to have a spelling bee. I'm going to sign up."

"Sugar Pie, since I taught you my secret spelling trick, you're a fantastic speller," Daddy says. "You should go right on ahead and sign up for that spelling bee."

"I think I will, Daddy!" I say. "I think it could be real fun."

Momma pours everyone sweet tea except me. I get pink lemonade. Y'all know pink is my color.

Everyone talks about their day. I stop and think about spelling each word I say. Ugly Brother hangs out under the table until I feel sorry for him and sneak him a tasty bite of dinner. Daddy winks at me. He sneaks Ugly Brother bites, too!

T.J. tells me, "If you're going to be in the bee, Lil' Bit, you better let a person help you study instead of our dog."

I say, "Shhh. Remember, he thinks he's a real true person!"

Ugly Brother barks, "Ruff, ruff!"

"Well, you hurt his feelings," I say. I eat fast. Then I say, "Can I be excused?"

"What are you going to do?" Momma asks.

I tell her, "I need to study more words!"

Chapter Five
Grocery Store Speller

Early, early Saturday morning Momma and I go
to do the grocery shopping at the Piggly Wiggly. In
the backseat, I spell words all the way there. I start
with an A word. Always. B word. Before. C word.
Crisp. I keep going till I get to Z for zoo!

When we finally get to the store we park in
the giant parking lot with the yellow stripes. It's
already half full of cars, vans, and trucks. Momma
waves to our neighbor Miss Clarabelle as she picks
a grocery cart.

Momma asks, "How are you, Miss Clarabelle? Your flowers sure are pretty this time of year."

Miss Clarabelle replies, "I'm fine. How are y'all doing? You know, I could use some help with my flowers. Maybe Kylie Jean can come help me pull some weeds later today."

Momma chooses a grocery cart. "We're all just fine. Thank you for asking," she says. Then she winks at me. "And Kylie Jean would be happy to help you weed your beautiful garden."

"Yes, I would!" I say.

First, Momma and I go to the fruits and vegetable section. I see lots of fruits and veggies. Big piles of pretty red tomatoes are stacked up, but I bet they don't taste as good as Pa's, fresh from the farm.

We finish in that part of the store lickety-split because we get most of our fruits and vegetables from Lickskillet Farm. Momma gets all of her herbs from Granny.

Next, we go to the butcher. He cuts the meat at the Piggly Wiggly. Momma gets hamburger, chicken, and steaks. She uses the steaks to make chicken fried steak, but they don't really have any chickens in them.

They have flour on the outside and Momma fries them in her big old black skillet. You can't flour a rich steak. Daddy cooks those on the grill!

After a while I get bored and say, "Hey, Momma, let's race!"

Momma shakes her head. "I don't think so," she says. "How about we play a game instead?"

"What kind of game?" I ask.

"A spelling game," Momma says.

That doesn't sound as fun as racing, but I'll give it a try. "Okay," I say.

As we walk along, putting canned goods, cereal, bread, and milk into the cart, Momma calls out words for me to spell. She says, "Spell dairy! And don't look at the sign!"

I spell, "D-a-i-r-y. Did I get it right?"

Momma cheers. "Yay! You did."

I tell her, "We like to say ta-da, not yay."

Momma says, "Okay, then, ta-da!"

She asks me to spell cereal, pie, and cupcake. All those words are on the second grade spelling bee practice list.

"Some of these words are pretty hard for a second grader," Momma says.

I nod. "Yes ma'am," I say. "That's why I need to practice all I can."

We keep loading up the cart and marking off our grocery list. In the cereal aisle, we really pile up the boxes. T.J. can eat a whole box in two days! I get a box of cereal with ABCs in it.

"Now you can practice while you eat your breakfast," Momma says.

Momma only shops every two weeks, so before long, we can hardly see because we have so many groceries piled up high.

Momma crosses off the last thing on her list. Then she says, "Come on, darlin'. We have one more aisle to go to before we check out."

This is so weird! I thought we finished the list.

We cross the store and turn down the pet aisle. Right in front of me is a whole section for cats.

They have cat food, cat toys, and cat collars. I see a pink collar!

I shout, "Oh, Momma, I just love that pink collar with the little diamonds and the big bow! Can I please buy it for Patches?"

"It sure is beautiful," Momma says. "But I'll have to take some money from your allowance. Okay?"I nod, holding the perfectly pink cat collar.

Momma says, "Now it's time to check out, sweet pea."

When we get to the front end, we go straight to Miss Bea's lane to check out. Miss Bea is real nice to me.

As Miss Bea scans our cans, I say, "Miss Bea, I'm going to be in a spelling bee."

"Are you really?" she asks.

Putting cereal boxes on the counter, I add, "I just said three Bs in one sentence: Bea, be, and bee."

Miss Bea stops scanning our groceries. "Aren't you something?" she says, smiling at me. "Can you spell orange?"

"No problem for me. I'm a fantastic grocery store speller," I brag.

After I spell orange, Miss Bea gives me a Piggly Wiggly sticker for each hand. After all, I had to spell a super hard word! Momma laughs and shouts, "Ta-da!"

Miss Bea scans the pink collar for Patches. I tell her, "That cat collar is for my new kitty, Patches. My cousin Lucy and I are her new mommas because she lost her real momma."

"That's real nice," Miss Bea says. "Thank you for shopping at Piggly Wiggly."

Then we have to hurry home and put all the groceries away before Lucy and her momma, Aunt Susie, bring Patches over.

It's my turn to have the kitty. Lucy got the first week, so we could have time to explain to Ugly Brother all about how he was going to get a little cat sister.

"You're really gonna like your new cat sister," I tell Ugly Brother while we wait for Lucy. "She's real nice."

Ugly Brother doesn't look too sure. Then I say, "You have to look out for her just like T.J. looks out for me. Okay?"

Ugly Brother barks, "Ruff, ruff."

But he doesn't really sound like he means it. I don't know if he's ready for a sister. I sure hope he is nice to her today, because being a big brother is a very important job!

When Lucy and Aunt Susie come into the kitchen, Momma is putting away the last box of Fruity-O's.

"Hello!" Aunt Susie says. "We are bringing this baby cat back to its other momma."

I run over to grab Patches. Lucy hands her to me. I hold the kitty up and give her a little kiss. Patches licks my face. It tickles a little. Her tongue is kind of rough and scratchy.

Ugly Brother is under the kitchen table. I tell him, "Come say hi to your little sister."

He barks, "Ruff." Then he lies right down and closes his eyes. How rude! He's not sleeping.

Lucy is not sure what to think. She asks, "Does Ugly Brother know Patches is going to stay here tonight?"

I shrug and say, "Well, I told him more than once. Wait until you see the new collar I just bought for her!"

I hold up the collar and Lucy gushes, "Ooh! I love it!"

Momma and Aunt Susie have a nice visit while Lucy and I play with Patches. Momma says sisters always have things to talk about. I sometimes wish I had a sister, but being a cat's momma is pretty fun, too!

Chapter Six
Pull and Spell

Later that afternoon, Miss Clarabelle calls to see if I can come over and help in her garden. Momma says yes.

She finds Patches and me in the back yard. We are stretched out swinging in the hammock. Patches is purring, and I'm reading a book called How to take Care of Your Kitten.

Momma asks, "Sweet Pea, are you ready to go help Miss Clarabelle in her garden?"

"Yup!" I answer. Then I tumble out of the hammock. Patches flies out and lands in the soft grass. She starts meowing.

Ugly Brother sees me on the ground and runs over to play, but when he sees Patches, he barks.

I shout, "Ugly Brother, you be nice to your baby cat sister!" Then, in a quieter voice, I say, "It's not time to play right now anyway. We've got to go help pull weeds."

Ugly Brother puts his head down. He knows I don't like it when he's mean to Patches.

I hand Patches to Momma. "Can you babysit Patches while I go pull weeds?" I ask.

"I sure can," Momma says. Then she and Patches head inside.

I go into the garage and get my basket, my hat, and my pink gardening gloves. Then I walk over to Miss Clarabelle's.

She is working on the flower beds in her back yard. There is a big pile of weeds on the ground next to her. I push them over. Then I sit down by her, pulling on my gloves.

"Why, hello, Kylie Jean!" she says. "Thank you so much for coming over to help me."

Under the orange lilies are thin, tiny green sprouts. The best thing to do is pull them out carefully so you get the roots too. If you don't get the roots the weeds grow right back.

"I see you have some weeds here," I say, looking at her flowers.

Miss Clarabelle smiles. "Yes, I do," she says. "And you are just as sweet as sugar to come and help me."

That gives me a great idea. "Can we practice spelling while we pull weeds?" I ask.

Miss Clarabelle replies, "That's a marvelous idea. You help me and I'll help you. Can you spell flowers?"

I spell, "F-l-o-w-e-r-s. Flowers."

Once I get that one right we just keep right on pulling weeds and spelling words. I spell spider, ant, plant, leaf, daisy and dirt. My pile of weeds is getting really big.

Ugly Brother has been sniffing around. I call, "Ugly Brother, come and help us."

He runs over and I load my pile of weeds into the basket I brought over.

I tell him, "Take these weeds over to the trash pile. Okay?"

He barks, "Ruff, ruff." Then he picks up some of the weeds in his teeth and takes off. I see some of the weeds fall out of his mouth as he runs.

Miss Clarabelle notices too. She smiles at me and says, "Maybe carrying weeds is not the best job for Ugly Brother."

"He can't pull weeds, either." I remind her. "Remember how he tried to eat them the last time I helped you?"

Miss Clarabelle laughs. "Oh, my! How could I forget?" she says.

We talk about the spelling bee and then I tell her all about Patches.

Miss Clarabelle is a good listener. That's a good thing, because I'm a good talker. Ugly Brother listens too.

Miss Clarabelle asks, "When will it be your turn to take care of the baby cat?"

"It's my turn to be Patches's momma right now," I say. "Momma is babysitting her while I'm here helping you."

Suddenly I miss that baby kitty so much I just want to go home. Miss Clarabelle looks at me. "You must miss her," she says. She looks around. "I think we're about done here, Kylie Jean, and you've been a big help to me. Why don't you head home now?"

I hop up and run away, calling, "Goodbye, Miss Clarabelle!"

Fun at the Farm

After church on Sunday, the whole big family is meeting at the farm for dinner. Except for Ugly Brother. He is not getting along with his little cat sister, so he has to stay home. It just breaks my heart.

Before we leave, I tell him, "I've told you a hundred times that I don't love Patches better than you. Please don't be jealous, so you can come to the farm, too!"

Ugly Brother barks, "Ruff!"

He has started barking whenever Patches is around. Barking dogs and cats don't mix, so we have to leave him behind.

When we finally get to Nanny and Pa's, I pull off my church clothes as fast as I can. In two seconds flat, I'm dashing out to the barn in my play clothes.

"Lucy, you in here?" I call as I make my way into the dark, sweet-smelling barn.

"I'm back here," she yells. Lucy is at the end of the barn looking for something.

Some of the horses shift and make soft noises as I pass by the stalls. There's a new colt in the last stall. It is black with wobbly legs.

Lucy says, "Come help me look for our old baby buggy."

"Did you see the new little h-o-r-s-e?" I ask her. "What's Pa going to name it?"

Lucy looks confused at first. Then she says, "Oh, I get it! You're practicing for the spelling bee. I did see it! It's so cute. Maybe they could name it Midnight."

As I get closer to the back of the barn, Patches starts to meow. She climbs up on my shoulder. Her tiny claws are kind of sharp. I guess she hears Lucy talking and is trying to see her other momma.

"Okay, I'm here to help you look," I tell Lucy. "I think they should name that colt Licorice. Pa's favorite candy is licorice. What are we going to do with the buggy when we find it?"

Lucy points to a big purple bag on the ground. There are some baby doll clothes spilling out.

I spell, "C-l-o-t-h-e-s." Then I ask, "Are we going to play dolls?"

"No, silly!" Lucy exclaims. "Those are for our sweet little kitty, Patches. I know she wants to look really cute, so we're going to dress her up in style."

Patches meows loudly. She looks funny wearing her fancy collar in the barn .

Suddenly, I feel nervous. "Do you think she can get hurt when we change her clothes?" I ask Lucy. After all, my job as Patches's momma is to see to it that she never gets hurt or goes hungry.

"No way," Lucy says. "Daisy dresses her cat up all the time!"

Now I'm getting excited. I try to imagine our Patches in a precious pink baby doll dress.

"You know what?" I say. "She is going to look like a p-r-i-n-c-e-s-s all dressed up."

Just then I see a tiny corner of the pink baby buggy. It's poking out of one of the empty stalls on the other side of the barn.

Pointing, I shout, "There it is!"

Our old doll stroller is stuck under a bunch of junk. First, Lucy pulls on the buggy. After I put Patches down, I pull. Then we both pull together, trying hard to get it out.

Finally, the stroller rolls right on out. It shoots out so fast that we both fall down laughing.

A bunch of old junk tumbles out behind it. Old watering cans, pool floats, egg baskets, and milk pails litter the barn floor. I stand up and dust myself off.

"We better clean this m-e-s-s up before Nanny sees it!" I whisper.

Lucy nods. We start stacking up the junk and shoving it back in the stall. When everything is put away, I suddenly remember our kitty.

I spin around and look at the spot where I put her down. It is just a dab of dirt without any little white fluffball sitting on it.

I scream, "Where's Patches?"

"I thought you were taking care of her!" Lucy says.

"I was," I say sadly. "But I put her down to help you with the buggy."

Lucy calls, "Patches, Patches! Come here, sweet little kitty!"

I feel as bad as a dog without a bone. I'm a terrible cat mother! Patches is lost and I don't know where to look. All around us are big horses that could scare an itty bitty baby cat.

"Maybe she's hiding from the horses, and she's too scared to come out," I say. "We should check in some good hiding spots."

Lucy shouts, "You can't take your eyes off a baby. Do you think she could get out of the barn by herself?"

I shake my head. Now I want to cry!

Lucy says, "If you really loved Patches you wouldn't lose her!"

That makes me feel even worse.

Then I hear a faint little meowing sound.

"Shhh! Hear that?" I ask.

Lucy says, "It's coming from the junk pile!"

Patches's tiny face pops out of a watering can. We both dash over, but I get there first.

I gently pour Patches out of the can and give her a great big hug. "Thank goodness you're safe," I say, nuzzling her little face. "We thought you were lost, but since we found you, I am the happiest girl in the whole wide world!"

Lucy is just itching to get her hands on our cat. "Come on, Kylie Jean," she says. "It's my turn to love on her and you lost her, so give her to me!"

I feel real bad about losing Patches, so I hand her over to Lucy for some kisses.

After that, we dress our kitten in a little pink dress with white lace and bows all over it. It has a little bonnet to match and looks nice with Patches's special pink collar.

Lucy puts a baby blanket in the buggy for Patches. It is as soft as a spring cloud. Then we carefully put our baby cat in the buggy so we can go show her off.

The buggy bounces along the dirt path from the barn to the farmhouse with Patches peeking over the side to see what is going on.

Pa sees us coming. He hollers, "Well, what do we have here?" We push the buggy close so he can see better. When he peeks inside, Pa grins and his eyes twinkle with laughter. "That's a beautiful little cat baby!" he says.

"Yes sir, we know," I say. Then I remember my manners and add, "and thank you kindly."

"Are y'all taking good care of your baby?" Pa asks.

Lucy says, "Yes sir!"

Then we both push the buggy down the hill to show everyone else our little princess.

Chapter Eight
Bad Dog

Finally, the big day arrives! It's time for the class spelling bee! As soon as I wake up on Monday morning, I start practicing spelling my words for one last time. While brushing my teeth, I spell a word. "S-h-i-n-e." Then I ask, "Ugly Brother, am I right?" and he barks, "Ruff, ruff."

I put on my best pink dress. Downstairs, Momma brushes my hair. I spell a word, t-o-g-e-t-h-e-r, as I hold Patches in my lap.

Daddy says, "Fantastic, sugar pie!"

"Thank you, Daddy," I reply, smiling.

Momma says, "Put that cat down before you go to the table."

I set Patches on the floor. Then I pull up a chair at the kitchen table next to T.J. He is stuffing pancakes in his mouth. I sip some orange juice. Momma makes my pancakes look like ABCs. Then she spells a word on my plate. It says l-o-v-e!

Suddenly from under the table we hear, "Meow, meow, meow!" It sounds like Patches is in trouble!

I shout, "T.J., did you step on my baby cat?"

T.J. looks shocked and says, "Hey, I didn't do it!"

I jump out of my chair and look for Patches. Peering under the table, I see Ugly Brother, but I don't see Patches.

Then I hear a meow that sounds like a whisper. Where is my baby cat? That's when I notice that Ugly Brother has two tails, and one is long and white!

"Oh no!" I yell. "Ugly Brother is sitting on Patches. Help!" I try to grab Ugly Brother's legs and pull him up. "You're being a bad dog! Get up before you squish Patches!" I tell him.

T.J. grabs Ugly Brother by the collar, dragging him out from under the table. Patches looks up at me with big eyes and cries, "Meeooowww!" Momma kneels down beside me, picking up Patches.

"Is Patches okay?" I ask, trying hard not to cry.

Momma says, "She's not hurt. She's just scared."

T.J. shuts Ugly Brother in the laundry room. Momma looks at me and says, "Kylie Jean, I think you better let Patches live with Lucy. You can always go visit. Ugly Brother just can't get used to having a little sister."

Now I can't stop myself from crying.

T.J. says, "It's almost time for the bus."

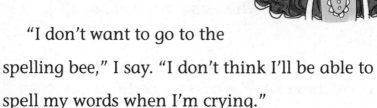

Daddy gives me a big squeezy hug. "Just calm down, sweetheart," he says.

"I don't want to go to the spelling bee," I say. "I don't think I'll be able to spell my words when I'm crying."

"Oh, hush," Daddy says. "You can do it."

"I have been practicing and practicing," I say, sniffling, "so I would hate to miss it."

Daddy smiles. "I have a prediction," he says. "You want to hear it?" I nod, and Daddy says, "You're gonna win that spelling bee today!"

Then I think of my poor little baby cat and I start to cry all over again. Ugly Brother could have hurt her really bad. Lucy would never forgive me!

I feel awful. Even though I'm still really sad, I grab my backpack, lunchbox, and homework. Then T.J. and I head outside to wait for the bus.

On the bus, I sit on the seat right behind Mr. Jim, our bus driver, so that I can tell him all about Ugly Brother sitting on Patches and today's spelling bee.

"Hey, Mr. Jim," I say. "My dog tried to sit on my cat! Today I'm going to be in my class spelling bee, but I'm so worried about Patches I don't know if I can remember how to spell my words."

Mr. Jim smiles. "I'm sorry about your cat," he says. "And good luck with your spelling bee."

"Oh, I don't need luck," I say. "I know all the words. Do you want me to spell them all for you right now?"

From the back of the bus, T.J. shouts, "Mr. Jim, please just say no. She really means it!"

Mr. Jim nods. "That's okay, Kylie Jean," he says. "I believe you can spell them all."

Chapter Nine
Class Bee

When we get to school, I go straight to my classroom. I have to tell Lucy about Ugly Brother and Patches. Maybe she'll be happy since our baby is going to have to live at her house.

As soon as I walk into the room, Lucy asks, "How is our baby cat?"

I take a deep breath. "Well, she's okay now," I say. "But Ugly Brother sat on her today! Please don't be mad. She's not hurt too bad, just scared."

Lucy gasps. "Are you sure she's okay?" she asks.

I reply, "Yup, cross my heart. And the good news is, Momma says Patches has to live at your house all the time now."

Lucy grins. "Well, you can come see her whenever you want," she says. "She'll always be your kitten too."

I smile. Lucy really is my best cousin.

"Are you ready for the spelling bee?" she asks.

I tell her, "I know all my words by heart."

After the bell rings, it's time to start the bee. My tummy is full of hummingbirds. I try to take deep breaths while I wait for my first word.

Ms. Corazón says, "Kylie Jean, please spell 'sister.'"

Sister is a great word because Ugly Brother has a little sister kitty now. Even if he doesn't like her. I say, "S-i-s-t-e-r."

Daisy gets "orange." It is kind of a hard word. Some kids think the g is a j, and Daisy gets it wrong. Ms. Corazón says, "I'm sorry, Daisy. You are out. Please sit down."

Cara gets "shape." She spells it right. I want to shout, "Ta-da!"

Next Lucy spells "S-m-a-r-t." She is so smart, she gets her word right.

I'm a little nervous. But you won't believe it — my next word is "kitten"! Of course I spell it right!

Cara gets "grandfather." I hold my breath for her. She spells "G-r-a-n-d-f-a-t-h-e-r."

Now it's Lucy's turn. Her word is "balloon."

She starts, "B-a-l . . ." but then she stops. She asks, "Can you please say the word again?"

Ms. Corazón says slowly, "Balloon."

Lucy takes a deep breath and spells, "B-a-l-o-o-n."

Ms. Corazón smiles kindly and says, "I'm sorry, Lucy. That was incorrect. Please sit down."

One by one, more students have to sit down. Soon, only Ryan and I are still standing. Ryan gets the word "between." It could be a hard one to spell, but he gets it right.

When it's my turn, I think of all the words I still don't know how to spell. Yikes! Luckily, I get the word "cookie."

Whew. That is a very easy Piggly Wiggly word. Being a grocery store speller helps me get it right. We are both still in the contest.

Ryan's next word is "hobby." He spells, "H-o-b-b-e-y." I want to jump up and down like a jack rabbit. He added an extra letter!

Ms. Corazón smiles at me and asks, "Kylie Jean, can you spell 'hobby' correctly? If you can, you'll be our class winner!"

I spell, "H-o-b-b-y."

"Correct!" Ms. Corazón exclaims. "You spelled your word with no mistakes. Now you will go on to the big bee on Monday with the all the students in first through fifth grade at our school."

I throw open my arms wide and shout, "Ta-da!"

My friends cheer, "Ta-da!"

Ms. Corazón pins a big blue ribbon to my shirt.
It says "First Place Speller" in gold letters. It's not a
tiara, but I like it!

I can't wait until after school so I can show Mr.
Jim, Momma, Daddy, T.J., and Ugly Brother my
big blue ribbon!

Chapter Ten
Some Speller

That afternoon, when Mr. Jim sees my first place spelling bee ribbon, he says, "Congratulations! You must be some speller, little lady."

"Yes sir, thank you very much," I say. "And now I'm going to be in the big spelling bee next Monday."

At home, I show Ugly Brother. I know I should be mad at him because he was mean to Patches, but I love him too much.

Besides, he is real proud of me and he wants to lick my ribbon. I tell him, "No licking the ribbon!" but I let him lick my face and give me some sugar.

Momma makes a special afternoon snack for me because I'm the winner. She says, "Blueberry Pop-Tarts for a blue ribbon winner."

We are still in the kitchen talking about being blue ribbon winners when Daddy comes home from work. He sneaks a bite of my Pop-Tart. I say, "Hey, that's my snack!"

Then he sees my big ole first place blue ribbon and says, "See, Sugar Pie, I knew you were going to be a fantastic speller!" Then he gives me a big squeezy hug.

"Your prediction came true, Daddy," I say.

Then Daddy spells, "P-r-e-d-i-c-t-i-o-n."

* * *

The next day is Saturday. As soon as I wake up, I pin my first place ribbon on my shirt. Downstairs, Momma is fixing cereal.

"Aww, I thought you were making eggs and bacon for breakfast today," T.J. complains.

Momma shakes her head. "Tomorrow I'm making a big breakfast," she explains, "so today we're having cereal."

She puts a box of Fruity-Os and a gallon of milk in front of T.J.'s bowl. I see that Momma already has a bowl of ABCs cereal ready for me.

"Thanks, Momma!" I say. "I love to eat alphabets! Yum!"

After I eat my breakfast, I spend all day practicing my spelling. I can play and practice at the same time. When I jump rope, I call out letters each time my feet skip over the rope. I jump and call out letter D, jump and call out letter R, jump and call out letter E, jump and call out letter A, jump and call out letter M.

Ugly Brother watches me. I tell him, "I just spelled 'dream.' You know that ever since I was an itty bitty baby it's been my dream to be a beauty queen."

He barks, "Ruff, ruff." I lay down the rope and give Ugly Brother my best beauty queen wave, nice and slow, from side to side.

I love my baby cat Patches, but now it's just like the old days, just me and Ugly Brother.

I use my sidewalk chalk to spell all the big words I have been learning on the driveway. I write the really big words with my pink chalk.

When T.J. comes home from football practice, he can tell I'm ready for the big bee. He says, "Looks like you're ready to spell."

I grin and spell, "Y-u-p!" The letters tumble right off my tongue and T.J. laughs.

After T.J. goes inside, I ask Ugly Brother, "Do you think I can win the big bee?"

He barks, "Ruff, ruff!"

That means yes!

Chapter Eleven

The Big Bee

On Monday morning, I am ready! I have on my lucky pink dress. As Momma kisses me goodbye, she says, "I know the big bee is from nine to eleven in the school auditorium. I'll be there!"

"Okay, Momma!" I say. "See you later!"

I am so excited that I can hardly sit still on the school bus. Mr. Jim looks in his rear-view mirror and says, "If I didn't know better, I'd think you were sittin' on a pile of fire ants, little lady!"

"Today is the big spelling bee and I'm in it," I remind him. "I even wore my lucky pink dress just in case I need some luck."

"Betcha won't need it," Mr. Jim says.

When we get to school, Cara, Paula, and my best cousin Lucy are waiting for me. Ms. Corazón is letting them help me practice one last time before the bee.

We go to the playground and swing and spell. They ask me the words.

When I get them right, my friends say, "Ta-da!"

Lucy says, "Spell family."

I spell, "F-a-m-i-l-y"

My friends all shout, "Ta-da!"

We keep on practicing. I spell owl, planet, spin, bread, jump, uncle, globe, and sheep.

Then Ms. Corazón comes to the door. She shouts, "Come in, girls! It's spelling bee time."

We yell, "Okay." Then we jump out of our swings and run for the door.

It's nine o'clock on the dot. Ms. Corazón leads our class into the auditorium so we can sit with all of the other second grade students in the two front rows. Then she helps me fix the bow on my pink dress. It must have come loose when I was wiggling on the bus.

Ms. Corazón tells me, "Win or lose, all I can ask is that you do your very best, Kylie Jean."

I take a deep breath. Then I reply, "Yes ma'am, you know I will. And when I do, I'll be as happy as a pig in mud!"

All of the contestants line up to go on the stage. I find my seat. It has a white paper taped to the back with my name on it, Kylie Jean Carter. I sit right on down. The chair is kind of tall and my feet swing back and forth.

I am a little anxious to get started. Next to me, Billy Joe from first grade looks like he just swallowed a bug. I decide I should tell him my teacher's advice. I give him a thumbs up and whisper, "You're gonna be just fine. Win or lose, just do your best."

He looks like he feels a little better. Then our principal welcomes everyone and now I know we're about to get started. I look out into the dim auditorium and I can barely see Momma in the audience. I give her a quick little beauty queen wave, side to side. Then I put my hands back in my lap.

I whisper to Billy Joe, "Did you know they don't like dogs to come to school even if they're your brother?" He looks shocked!

One of the teachers, Ms. Shay, will call out the words. After she says the word, you can ask her to say it again or say the definition.

Ms. Shay gives me the word "sailboat." I ask her to say it again while I try to remember if it's one long word. Then I spell, "S-a-i-l-b-o-a-t."

She says, "Correct!"

Other kids spell their words. Then Billy Joe gets his word. His word is "green." He goes and gets it right.

Ms. Shay says, "Correct!"

Beside me, Billy Joe gives a great big sigh. "Whew."

The round is over. All of us got our first word right.

In the next round, the third grader misses her word and is out. Poor Billy Joe gets his word wrong and is out, too. He looks like he's going to cry. That means it's just me and two other kids.

My word is "whiskers." It is a strange word. What if I get it wrong? I'll be out of the bee!

Then I remember the cute kitty's picture on Patches's bag of cat food. Suddenly, I can see the word in my mind.

I get it right, and I'm still in the contest! After all, I did practice at the Piggly Wiggly. I'm a real true grocery store speller, so I know my food words.

Momma claps and cheers, "Ta-da!"

We start the next round. The fourth grader gets his word, "wobble," right. The fifth grader gets the word "yesterday." It's a long one, so she takes her time. I can see her chewing her lip. She is thinking hard before she spells it. Once she does, she gets it right.

I get the word "horse." I am lucky because I love horses. Of course I get my word right.

The fourth grader gets the word "nickel." He says, "N-i-c-k-l-e—" Then he covers his face with his hands. He knows he spelled it wrong. Up until he mixed up the last two letters, he had it right. I think he was just nervous!

Now the fifth grader stands up.

Ms. Shay says, "Please spell 'opposite.'"

The fifth grader spells, "O-p-p-o-s-i-t, opposite."

That sounds right to me, but Ms. Shay says, "I'm sorry, that is incorrect. If Kylie Jean can spell the word, she is the winner."

I blurt out, "I bet I can spell that word!"

Ms. Shay says, "Go ahead, Kylie Jean, and spell opposite for us."

I stand up tall, thinking about the sneaky e like at the end of the word "people." That has to be the mistake that fifth grader made.

I call my letters out as loud as I can. "O-p-p-o-s-i-t-e, opposite."

"I just left out one letter?" the fifth grader says. He moans. "No fair."

Ms. Shay turns to the audience and announces, "We have a new spelling bee champion, second grader Kylie Jean Carter! She will represent our school in the county-wide spelling bee at the end of the month."

She presents me with a beautiful trophy.

It is a golden cup with ABCs around the bottom and on the front it says "Big Bee, Spelling Winner." It looks like a tall cup with handles on both sides. It is not a tiara, but I like it anyway.

Everyone in second grade is chanting my name. "Kylie Jean! Kylie Jean!"

Momma is waiting beside the stage to give me a big squeezy hug. I hold up the trophy so Momma can see. She laughs. "Kylie Jean, you are a super speller."

I say, "Ta-da! I knew I could do it, Momma!"

* * *

When I get home that afternoon, I run all the way from the bus to the front door as fast as I can!

After I slam the front door, I holler, "Ugly Brother, come quick! Ugly Brother!" He runs toward me. We sit together on the floor by the front door so that I can show him my spelling bee trophy. Ugly Brother sniffs it and licks the outside of it.

"Don't you just love my ABC spelling bee trophy?" I ask.

He barks, "Ruff, ruff!" Then he tries to fit his nose inside the trophy cup.

I know just what he's thinkin'. I laugh. "Silly Ugly Brother! We can share this trophy, but no eating out of it! Okay?"

Ugly Brother barks, "Ruff, ruff."

Then I add, "We're gonna share this trophy with Miss Clarabelle, T.J., Momma, and Daddy. They all helped me learn to spell."

I pet Ugly Brother and he licks my face. That means he likes my idea. Sharing makes a person good on the outside and on the inside. Just like Momma always tells me, pretty is as pretty does.

"Ugly Brother, I sure wish they had spelling bee queens," I say. "Can you spell queen?"

He barks once, "Ruff." That means no.

I spell, "Q-u-e-e-n."

Ugly Brother barks twice and licks my face. "Yup! That's me," I say. "Kylie Jean, the Spelling Bee Queen!"

Kylie Jean

Cupcake Queen

Table of Contents

Chapter One
Saturday Sales

On Saturday mornings, my favorite thing to do is go to garage sales! As soon as I wake up, I get excited. Today I get to go with Momma, Granny, and Pappy. I love garage sales!

I look out my window and notice that the sky is streaked with gray, gold, and pink. Then I notice something else. Granny and Pappy are already parked in front of our house on Peachtree Lane, waiting for me and Momma. I bet Pa's rooster hasn't even crowed yet.

I better hurry up! If I take too long, Pappy will honk the horn and wake up Miss Clarabelle, my neighbor.

I hurry to get dressed. Momma calls, "Kylie Jean, are you ready to go yet?"

"Almost," I yell. "Don't leave without me. Okay?"

I just need my pink purse. It's not anywhere in my room. When I go downstairs, Ugly Brother is waiting by the front door.

I ask, "Did you see my purse?"

He barks, "Ruff."

One bark means no.

If I have to go to the sales without any money, it won't be much fun.

"Come on, Kylie Jean," Momma calls from the kitchen. "Granny and Pappy are waiting."

"Ugly Brother, please, please help me look for it!" I beg.

Then I see something pink poking out from under his tail, so I run over and pull out my purse. It has a sparkly cupcake on the front.

"Ugly Brother!" I yell. "Were you lying to me?"

He whines and lies down on the floor. He looks sad. Then I realize why he hid my purse.

"You don't want me to leave, do you, boy," I say, giving him a pat.

Ugly Brother agrees. "Ruff, ruff!"

I grab my purse. When I shake it, I can tell there's money inside, so I don't need to go back to my room and get money from my piggy bank. A girl has to have money to go shopping, right?

"Ready, Momma!" I say. She walks into the living room and we head outside.

Momma slides across the giant back seat of Pappy's old-timey car. I scoot in beside her.

Momma announces, "Sorry, everybody. We're running late because Kylie Jean lost her purse again."

Pappy laughs. "It always takes that pretty little girl a while to get ready," he says. "I was getting ready to honk, but then you came on out."

Granny asks, "Who's hungry for pancakes?"

"I'm so hungry for pancakes I could eat a full stack all by myself!" I say.

Pappy smiles. "Okay, first pancakes, then garage sales," he says.

Before I know it, we're pulling in to the Pancake Palace. It's a funny building that looks like a castle. Outside, it is covered with stone. It has heavy wood doors and a tower with a tiny window. Inside, the floor is red and white like a checkerboard, and the tables are red, too.

We sit down. Our waitress comes to take our order right away. "How are y'all?" she asks. "What are you having today? Coffee, right?"

I say, "We're peachy keen, and today I'm a garage sale queen. I would like a short stack and juice, please, ma'am."

Momma, Pappy, and Granny all order their breakfasts. Our waitress scratches it all down on a notepad with her pencil, and then disappears into the kitchen. Faster than you can say "flapjacks," she comes back with a tray loaded down with our food.

My plate is piled high with pancakes. I pour syrup all over the top of my pancakes, and it runs down over the edge of the plate and onto the table.

"Oops!" I exclaim.

Momma dips her napkin in her water glass and hands it to me. She says, "Wipe up that mess right away, Kylie Jean, or you'll be too sticky to go to garage sales."

It's quiet while we eat. We are all too busy chewing to do much talking!

Once Pappy and I are done eating, he leans over and whispers, "If you're going to garage sales, you gotta have a plan." Then he shows me the sale ads in the paper.

Using a pink marker, we circle the ones that say "huge" or "big sale." Sometimes more than one family or even a group like a church will have a sale. You have to know the best neighborhoods for sales, too. Some places only have junk, and you want to find the really good stuff.

We map out our route and load into the car. We are ready to shop, shop, shop!

At the first sale, Momma gets a fancy new dress with the tags still on it for five dollars.

While she pays, I notice that there's a boy selling ice-cold water in bottles for one dollar each. It is already hot out, so lots of people are buying water while they wait to pay.

In the car, Momma says, "Wasn't that little boy selling water cute?"

"He was a born salesman," Granny says. "He asked everyone who walked up to buy water."

The next sale is on River Road.

Granny digs through a box of junky jewelry and buys an old necklace for fifty cents. After she pays, Granny puts the necklace in the palm of my hand. I like the sparkly fake diamonds on it. They twinkle like stars in a night sky.

As we leave, I see that at this sale, there's a boy sitting behind a card table. He's selling some watery pink Kool-Aid for fifty cents a cup. His pitcher has flies buzzing around it. Ick! Flies remind me of Pa's cow pasture.

On Dogwood Street, Pappy buys an old camera for two dollars. A little bitty girl and her big sister are out front selling lemonade for twenty-five cents.

Granny tells the girls, "You sure do have a good price on your lemonade. I'll take a cup."

The sister helps the tiny girl pour Granny a cup. We head to the car.

Granny takes a sip and makes a terrible scrunched-up face. She cries, "They forgot to put the sugar in this! It's so sour, it will curl your hair."

The last sale we go to is at my friend Cara's house. I find the cutest orange stuffed kitten for a dollar.

I show the little kitty to Momma. "Isn't this little cat adorable?" I ask.

Momma doesn't say anything because she does not want me to have any more stuffed animals. I count out all of my change and Cara helps me count, too. I only have sixty-eight cents.

"Please, Momma, can I borrow some money?" I ask sweetly. "I just need a little bit more. I can pay you back when we get home."

Momma shakes her head. "No way, little lady," she says. "You have too many stuffed toys already!"

Pappy says, "I'll lend you the money. If you'll make me a promise."

"Okay," I say. "I'll do anything for this cute little kitten!"

Pappy looks me in the eye and asks, "Do you promise to give away one of your stuffed animals to your cousin Lucy?"

Right away, I agree. "Yup! I promise." Then he grins and gives me a loan.

Borrowing money is not easy. I think I better get my very own job. Then I can buy any ol' thing I want!

As we are leaving, I see sodas in a cooler full of ice. There's a sign that says, "Cokes for $1.50 each."

Cara asks, "Do you want to buy some Cokes?"

"They sure do look icy cold, sweet, and delicious!" I say, glancing at Pappy.

"We'll take four of those drinks," Pappy says, handing Cara six dollars. "Here you go!"

Cara is getting RICH! And she's not the only one. At almost every sale there has been a kid out front selling something! I need to get a business, too!

Chapter Two
Teatime Treats

On Sunday, we go to church, but we don't go to Lickskillet Farm for Sunday dinner afterward. Instead, we're going to a tea party at Miss Clarabelle's! Lucy gets to come, too.

Miss Clarabelle sent us a fancy invitation and everything. The invitation had pink roses on it and smelled like roses, too. We had to R.S.V.P., which means telling her if we are coming or not.

On the way home from church, Lucy and I sit all the way in the back of the van so we can have a little chat. T.J. sits in the middle. Daddy and Momma sit in the front.

I ask Lucy, "Did you know kids can get rich?"

"I never thought about it much," she says. "How do they do it?"

T.J. turns around and says, "They probably have to get a real job like me."

"They were not mowing lawns," I say. "They were selling stuff to drink at garage sales."

I explain all about the water, Kool-Aid, lemonade, and sodas.

"So that's how I figured out I need to start a business," I tell Lucy.

"What kind of drinks are you going to sell?" she asks.

I shake my head. "I like to be different, so I don't want to sell stuff to drink," I explain.

Lucy raises an eyebrow. She says, "We have all afternoon to think of something."

I know she's right. Pa always says that two heads are better than one.

When we pull in to our driveway, Ugly Brother is sitting right in the middle of it waiting for us. I think he would like to go with us on Sundays, but Momma says dogs do not belong in church.

As we climb out of the van, Momma warns us, "You girls, don't go gettin' all dirty before your tea party."

We say, "Yes, ma'am!"

We can hardly wait until two o'clock for teatime. But we have things to do before the party. First we all sit down at the kitchen table for some leftover fried chicken and potato salad for lunch.

When we're done eating, I ask, "Is it time yet?"

Momma says, "No. Run along and play. I'll call you when it's time."

Lucy, Ugly Brother, and I go upstairs so Lucy can pick out one of my stuffed animals to take home. I promised Pappy I would give her one, and I always keep my promises.

In my room, Lucy looks at dogs, bunnies, kittens, bears, an elephant, and a pink pony. She says, "I sure do like this pony, but you probably want to keep it."

She keeps on looking. Finally she finds a cute little turtle. "Can I have this one?" she asks.

"Yup!" I say.

We play for a while. Then we hear Momma holler that it's time for tea. We jump up, fluffing out the skirts of our church dresses. My dress is pink with white trim and fluffy sleeves. I'm going to wear my little white gloves, too. Lucy has on a polka-dot dress.

Downstairs, Ugly Brother also wants to go to the tea party, but he is not invited. Momma says bringing an extra guest is rude. Poor Ugly Brother! He has been stuck at home all day!

Lucy and I cross Miss Clarabelle's yard, being extra careful not step on her pretty flowers.

On the porch, there is a fancy iron table set
with a polka-dot tablecloth. On top of the table
there's a sparkly glass vase full of pink roses.

I say, "I bet those roses are from Miss
Clarabelle's garden."

When we get closer, I can see the teapot with
little pink flowers on it and the little teacups.

"Ooh la la!" Lucy whispers. "This is a fancy party."

I ring the doorbell. Miss Clarabelle comes to the door carrying a silver tray.

"Well, good afternoon, young ladies," she says. "I am so glad you could come for tea."

"Good afternoon," Lucy whispers.

I add, "Thank you for inviting us."

Miss Clarabelle asks, "Can one of you hold the door, please?"

I swing the door open and Miss Clarabelle puts the tray on the table. We follow her. She says, "Please have a seat and I will be right back."

The tray has teeny tiny cucumber and chicken salad tea sandwiches. Yum!

There is also a plate of juicy red strawberries and glistening green grapes.

Lucy says, "Everything looks so tasty."

I agree, "Yup."

Then we don't talk much. And that's weird for me and Lucy. Usually we're talking all the time! That tells you this tea is real special.

When Miss Clarabelle joins us, she's carrying a little silver stand with cookies shaped like teapots and tiny pink cupcakes. She notices my white gloves and says, "Kylie Jean, ladies remove their gloves for tea."

I slip my gloves off as Miss Clarabelle sits down. Then I ask, "Ma'am, are there other rules for having tea?"

Miss Clarabelle says, "Oh my, yes! Would you like to learn about them?"

"Yes, ma'am!" we exclaim.

She tells us all about the tea rules.

Tea Etiquette

1. Ladies always remove their gloves before enjoying tea.

2. Ladies put their napkins in their laps.

3. The hostess always pours tea once the guests are seated.

4. Ladies stir their tea gently, careful not to tap the sides of the cup.

5. Ladies do not stick out their pinky fingers while drinking tea.

Now that we know our tea manners, we are ready for tea.

First we put milk and sugar in our teacups. Miss Clarabelle pours the tea from her momma's china teapot. She is careful not to fill our cups too full. Then she looks at me and says, "Please pass the tea sandwiches."

The silver tray is heavy, but I do my best. She puts two tea sandwiches on her plate. Lucy and I do the same. Then we pass the sweets around.

I ask, "May I please have two cookies?"

Miss Clarabelle replies, "Yes, since you asked so nicely."

Lucy asks, "Then may I please have two cookies, too?"

Miss Clarabelle smiles and agrees. We each add a cupcake to our plate and then it's finally time to eat.

Lucy takes a big bite of her cookie and mumbles, "This cookie is scrumptious."

I remind her, "Momma says don't talk with your mouth full."

Lucy swallows and says, "Sorry." I smile at her so she won't feel embarrassed.

We keep eating our delightful treats. My favorite things are the strawberry cream cupcakes. The frosting is so sweet and creamy. They are just delicious!

"It's nice of you to come to tea," Miss Clarabelle says. "Sometimes I get so lonely in this old house."

We smile. "Thanks for inviting us," I say. "Tea parties are fun!"

"What have you girls been doing lately?" Miss Clarabelle asks.

I explain all about my plan to start a business.

"What a wonderful idea!" Miss Clarabelle says. "It's important for young women to learn about business."

Lucy says, "Now she just has to think of something to sell."

Just then, an idea hits me faster than buttercream frosting on red velvet cake! I'm going to sell cupcakes!

Chapter Three
In Business

I can't wait to tell Momma and Ugly Brother all about my plan to sell cupcakes!

After we're done with our tea party, Lucy and I thank Miss Clarabelle for inviting us. Then we skip all the way across the yard.

At my house, Aunt Susie is already here to pick up Lucy. She and Momma are having coffee in the kitchen.

As we walk in, Aunt Susie says, "Well, don't you girls look sweeter than sugar."

Momma laughs and says, "They're probably full of sugar! Miss Clarabelle is a fabulous baker."

"Did you girls have fun?" Aunt Susie asks. "How was tea?"

We tell them all about the sandwiches, teapot cookies, and yummy cupcakes. Momma looks at Aunt Susie and says, "I think we should have had tea instead of coffee. Those treats sound delicious!"

"Tea is better than coffee," I say.

"Especially with lots of milk and sugar!" Lucy adds, giggling.

After they leave, I tell Momma all about my plan. When I'm done talking, Momma thinks for a minute. Then she says, "Kylie Jean, I love the idea of you starting a business. But you'll need to invest your own money in it."

"What does that mean?" I ask nervously. I don't have very much money.

"That means you'll use your allowance to buy ingredients," Momma explains.

Ugly Brother and I run upstairs to dump my piggy bank and count the change.

There are lots of quarters, dimes, and pennies, and some paper money. I count all the coins, stacking them up into little piles. I put four quarters in each stack so they are each worth a dollar.

Ugly Brother tries to sniff the stacks.

"No, Ugly Brother!" I shout. "You better let me count them before you knock them over."

He barks, "Ruff, ruff."

There are ten one-dollar bills, a five-dollar bill, and a ten-dollar bill. With all of my coins, I have thirty dollars.

Wow! I'm already rich!

Looking at all my money, I realize I've been saving it for something special, and this is it! And once I make more money, I can buy anything I want when I go shopping.

I run downstairs to tell Momma. She's in the kitchen, talking to T.J.

"I have thirty dollars!" I shout.

T.J. asks, "Can I borrow some money?"

"No way!" I say. "I need all my money to buy the ingredients for my cupcake business."

"You should make chocolate cupcakes," T.J. says.

"Hmm," I say. "Momma, what kind do you think I should make?"

Momma thinks for a minute. "My favorite is red velvet with cream cheese frosting," she says. "But Daddy's favorite is lemon. And I know you like vanilla best, right?"

"That's right," I say.

I think about it a little bit more. "I also like strawberry, because they're pink," I add. "If I make everybody's favorite, I could have four flavors. Or should I do more?"

"Four flavors is plenty," Momma tells me.

"Where are you going to sell your cupcakes?" T.J. asks.

My mouth falls open. Oh no! My plan to start my own business will fall apart unless someone has a garage sale!

Chapter Four
Hello, Cupcake!

The next afternoon, I am busy making myself an after-school snack when Daddy comes into the kitchen. He says, "Hello, cupcake!"

Grinning, I say, "Hello, Daddy!" Before he can say anything else, I decide to tell him about my problem. "I need someone to have a garage sale so I can sell my cupcakes. Can you pretty please have one? Oh, and can it be this Saturday?"

Daddy laughs. "That's not much time to get ready for a big sale."

"I can help get everything ready," I say. "Ugly Brother can help, too!"

Ugly Brother whines and puts his paws over his head. I lower my voice and tell him, "I think you are starting to be a big ol' lazy bones!" When he hears me say "bones," he barks. I'm not sure if he is barking because he is lazy or hungry.

Daddy looks at me. "Let's talk to your momma over dinner and see what she thinks," he suggests. "Okay, cupcake?"

I nod. "Yes, sir."

We are having spaghetti and meatballs for dinner. Ugly Brother only likes the meatballs, because the noodles stick to his tongue. That makes them hard for him to eat.

Momma lets me put the silverware on the table and fold the napkins. When I'm done, she hugs me and says, "This table looks amazing!"

T.J. comes in, sniffing the air. "And somethin' smells amazin'!" he says. "What's for dinner?"

I tell him, "Spaghetti and meatballs, bread, and salad. Yummy!"

We all take our seats around the big table. Daddy says grace and we dig in.

T.J. loads up. He has a little mountain of pasta noodles and meatballs on his plate. Momma passes the salad and bread.

Everything is delicious.

We are so busy eating that I almost forget to bring up the big garage sale!

Luckily, Daddy remembers.

"Why don't we have a big garage sale this weekend?" he asks Momma. "The weather is going to be just right."

Momma raises an eyebrow. "I'm sure Kylie Jean put you up to this so she can sell cupcakes," she begins. Then she sighs and says, "But that garage needs a good cleanin', so I say let's do it."

"Yay!" I shout. Ugly Brother and T.J. both groan.

After dinner, we spend all evening cleaning out the garage! I'm getting tired and there are a lot of skeeters out, but the garage is full of junky treasure.

First we push all the boxes to one side of the garage. Then we start opening them to see what's inside. It's fun, like a real treasure hunt!

Momma finds a box of old baby stuff. It has sippy cups, bottles, baby toys, blankets, and clothes.

"Were those things mine or T.J.'s?" I ask.

Momma says, "They're all pink, so they must have been yours."

"Aww," I say, looking at a teeny tiny dress. "I was such an itty bitty baby."

"You sure were," Momma says. "And some other momma will love to buy these sweet clothes and other baby things for her little girl."

Daddy and T.J. find a big box of old coins and stamps. When he was a little kid, T.J. collected that kind of stuff.

Daddy thinks someone will buy them. He finds some tools to sell, too. We're finding lots of things to sell!

Piles of stuff are everywhere. I can't even see Ugly Brother.

I call him and he barks, wiggling out of a pile of coats.

Momma is sorting and organizing the piles. One big pile is just trash.

Daddy starts loading all of the trash into the back of his truck to take to the city dump, and T.J. helps him.

"You and Ugly Brother could go to your room and pick out some of your old toys to sell at the garage sale," Momma tells me. "You can keep the money from any of your toys that sell."

"Okay," I shout, clapping my hands. Ugly Brother and I run to my room. Well, I run. Ugly Brother doesn't.

Choosing toys to sell turns out to be a lot harder than I thought it would be! I pick out some dollies, but I want to keep them all. I lay all them on my bed and look at them. I finally decide to sell my lemon cupcake cutie doll.

Ugly Brother brings me a purple stuffed bear.

"Okay, we can sell that bear," I agree. "What other animals can we sell? Not my pony. Okay, Ugly Brother?"

Ugly Brother barks, "Ruff, ruff." Then he brings me a rainbow fish, a little gray mouse, a pink kitty, and a green frog. I don't really want to sell them, but I put them in the pile anyway.

Ugly Brother helps me put them all in a box, and we take them down to the garage.

When Momma looks in the box, she exclaims, "I am so proud of you for choosin' some toys to sell in the sale. Good job!"

I say, "Thank you, Momma."

Momma checks her watch. "You have to go to school tomorrow," she says. "It's bedtime."

While I get ready for bed, I think about all of the great stuff we found to sell. After I climb up in the bed and pull the covers all around me, Ugly Brother jumps up and scoots up right beside me so we are snug as two bugs in a rug.

All night long, I dream about making cupcakes. I bake them and frost them with fluffy white icing. They are not plain old cupcakes. Instead, I put little doggie bone treats on the top. Ugly Brother eats them up!

When I wake up, I have a new idea! I'm not just gonna make cupcakes for people. My business will sell cupcakes for dogs, too!

Chapter Five
Cupcake Queen

When I get to school, I go straight to my classroom and sit down at the table I share with Cara, Paula, and Lucy.

I can't wait to tell Paula and Cara about my cupcake plan. Lucy already knows all about it, except for the doggie cupcake part.

I announce, "I am going into the bakery business and sellin' cupcakes! All kinds of cupcakes — even some for doggies!"

The girls gush, "Ohhh!"

"You must be so excited," Cara says.

"Yup," I say, adding, "I'm startin' my own business so I can get rich! Momma and I are startin' the bakin' tonight."

Paula looks puzzled. "You know dogs don't buy cupcakes, right?" she says. "Are your cupcakes going to be free? Because sellin' things to dogs is a bad plan if you're trying to get rich."

"No, silly," I say. "The people who own the dogs will buy the cupcakes."

"Oh," she says. "I get it." But she doesn't look too sure.

All morning, it seems like the clock is stuck! The time passes by slower than the roller coaster line at the state fair.

When the clock finally says eleven, it is time for lunch. Usually we bring our lunch, but today they are having corn dogs. Nothing tastes better for lunch than a nice hot corn dog covered in ketchup.

The lunch room is big and has rows and rows of brightly colored round tables. It's so noisy! You have to yell or no one can hear you.

While my friends and I wait in line, I see some kids with Popsicles on their tray. Pointing, I shout, "Hey, it's lucky Popsicle tray day."

Lucky Popsicle tray day is amazing! Some kids who buy their lunches get FREE Popsicles on their trays. I just know Lucy will get one. She is luckier than a four-leaf clover.

Sure enough, she gets a pink one. Well, you know pink is my color and I have the best cousin in the whole wide world because she wants to give her Popsicle to me.

Lucy hands it over, saying, "You take it, Kylie Jean. Look, it's your favorite flavor — pink lemonade."

I am so excited about my cupcakes I can't even eat it, so I say, "No thanks, Lucy," and give it back. Lucy stuffs the Popsicle into her mouth before she eats her corn dog and fries.

I laugh, and she smiles at me with her pink Popsicle mouth.

Normally I just love recess, but today even recess takes a long, long time. I can't wait to test out cupcake recipes with Momma. I just know they'll come out de-li-cious!

Momma is a blue-ribbon baker. Every year she wins prizes at the fair. Besides, just the way folks eat up her good food tells you she is the best cook in the county. Maybe even the whole state of Texas! She is gonna help me make the best cupcakes ever.

When we get back to our classroom, the rest of the day goes by slower than molasses in January. Finally, the last bell rings!

I grab my backpack and head for the door. It seems like the whole class is in line in front of me and they're all taking forever.

From the back of the line, I shout, "If y'all don't hurry up, some of us are going to miss our bus!" My complaining doesn't seem to rush them very much. Everyone likes to take their sweet time. They must not have cupcakes to bake.

We push through the crowded hallway and out the double doors into the sunshine. My bus is at the front of the line today. Yay for Mr. Jim! He is our bus driver. If he were a cupcake, he'd be chocolate cake because he has dark brown hair.

Jumping on the bus, I shout, "Hurry, Mr. Jim! Drive as fast as you can."

"Whoa, slow down," he says, wiping his face with his red bandana. "What's your big hurry anyway, gal?"

I explain, "Momma has an apron waiting for me and I need to get busy quick so I can sell a million cupcakes and be a cupcake queen!"

Mr. Jim looks surprised. I surprise him a lot, I think.

I slide into the seat right behind him and get busy doing my math problems. Usually I have a little chat with Mr. Jim, but not today.

I don't even ask him any math questions!

By the time we pick up the middle school kids, I am done with math and moving on to my spelling list. Right after we pick up T.J. and the high school kids, I finish all my homework.

Stuffing my book in my backpack, I shout, "Done!" Mr. Jim gives me a thumbs-up.

Soon we pull up in front of our house. As I get off the bus, I ask, "How many cupcakes do you want to buy, Mr. Jim?"

He says, "I might just have to buy a whole dozen. You're going to need to sell a lot of cupcakes to get to a million!"

Chapter Six
Bake-Off

Momma is in the kitchen getting ready to bake. She is wearing an apron with little pink and brown cupcakes all over the material.

I gush, "Oh, Momma, I just love your new apron!"

Momma smiles. "Turn around and close your eyes," she says. "I have something for you."

Momma slips an apron over my head. Then she ties it on with a big bow.

"Open your eyes," she says.

The apron looks just like Momma's. I smooth the front and whisper, "I love it! Where did you get it?"

"I told Granny about your new business," Momma says. "She made them for us. Now, let's get started!"

Cupcake recipes are laid out in neat rows on the kitchen table. Momma and I sit down to decide which ones to make.

It is a hard decision. Everyone likes chocolate and vanilla. Momma's favorite is red velvet. Strawberry and Italian cream cake are both good, too.

And I definitely want to make a special recipe Momma found for doggie cupcakes!

I ask, "How are we going to choose flavors?"

"You should make chocolate and vanilla, plus the dog recipe. Then choose two other flavors for variety," Momma suggests.

I choose strawberry because I like the pink frosting. Then I pick red velvet since most folks like it. I put the recipe cards next to the big bowl mixer.

"Which one is first?" I ask.

"Let's start with the chocolate," Momma decides.

We read the recipe carefully. Momma calls out the ingredients and I fetch them for her.

She lists, "Flour, sugar, butter, eggs, milk, cocoa, salt, baking powder, and vanilla."

I gather them up and tote them over to Momma.

First, we beat the golden butter until it is fluffy. I measure in the sugar as the mixer buzzes along.

Next comes the tricky part — cracking the eggs. Momma hands me a little bowl. Standing at the kitchen table, I tap the egg on the side of the bowl, watching a crack break across its middle. Pressing the sides of the egg, I hold my breath. I don't want the shell to break into the bowl along with the egg.

"Oh no!" I cry as I see little pieces of shell swirling in the egg.

Momma winks. "Try again, sweetie. It takes practice."

The bowl gets a rinse in the sink and I get another egg. This time the egg slides right out into the bowl with no shell. Yay!

But the recipe calls for two eggs. Can I do it again? Momma hands me another egg. I tap the egg, and success! It slips into the bowl, no shell. Momma adds them to the big mixing bowl. The beaters go buzz, buzz. The vanilla smells sweet when I carefully pour it into a measuring spoon.

I add flour and cocoa. The beaters are coated with fudgy goodness. It's starting to look pretty tasty, but we are too busy to try any.

Momma asks, "Can you put the cupcake liners in the pans?"

"Yes, ma'am," I say.

The cupcake liners stick together. I gently pull them apart and sort out the pink ones. Momma scoops the chocolate batter into the pretty pink paper cupcake liners, careful not to get any on the ruffled edges. Before you know it, that batch is in the oven and the kitchen smells yummy.

Time for a new batch! We rinse, wipe, wash, and get everything ready to start again.

The back door slams as T.J. comes in. "Where's my cupcake?" he asks.

"Sorry, these cupcakes are for my business," I tell him.

Then an idea hits me like candles on birthday cake! "If you want to earn a cupcake," I say, "you could do some work for me. I could pay you in cupcakes!"

T.J. laughs. "What do I have to do?" he asks.

"That's easy," I say. "Help us make cupcakes!"

T.J. always tries to make everything a contest. He says, "Let's have a bake-off to see who makes the best cupcakes!"

I make the strawberry, with light pink icing. Momma helps me a little, but she mostly makes her red velvet cupcakes, bakes the doggie cupcakes, and ices the chocolate cupcakes with red icing. T.J. makes vanilla, and a big mess! He has so much flour on him that he looks like a polar bear.

I put a doggie treat on top of one of the doggie cupcakes. "Why did you do that?" T.J. asks. "Nobody wants to eat a cupcake with a dog treat on it!"

"Dogs do!" I say. "I'm selling doggie cupcakes."

T.J. thinks about it for a minute. "You know, that's a pretty good idea," he says.

"I know!" I say proudly.

When Daddy comes home, we're still busy baking. He says, "This kitchen smells sweeter than a candy factory."

T.J. nods. "We're having a baking contest," he explains, "and you get to be the judge."

"Lucky me!" Daddy laughs. "Can Ugly Brother judge the ones with the dog bones on top?"

We all look at Ugly Brother. His tongue is hanging out of his mouth.

"I think he's counting on it," Momma says.

Ugly Brother is so excited about getting a cupcake that he chases his tail in a circle. Momma pours Daddy a tall glass of milk. She brings it to the table. Then I set three cupcakes on a pretty blue plate and carry them to Daddy.

I set the dog bone cupcake on the floor. Ugly Brother gobbles it up and barks, "Ruff, ruff!"

Daddy takes a big bite of each cupcake. Ugly Brother whines under the table.

Daddy says, "The winner is . . ."

You probably already guessed. Momma wins the bake-off!

Chapter Seven
Puppy Chow

The vanilla doggie bone cupcakes look good, and Ugly Brother has tried several. He loves them, but he eats anything. I wonder if other dogs will like them, too.

"Do you think other doggies will like my cupcakes?" I ask.

He barks, "Ruff."

One bark means no, but I do not believe him. He just wants to eat all the cupcakes.

Before I sell any cupcakes, I have to make sure other dogs will like them. Suddenly, an idea hits me like fleas on a dog. The Puppy Place Doggie Shelter is the perfect spot to bring cupcakes and find out if other doggies will like them.

So the next day after school, that's what my plan is! On the way home on the bus, I tell Mr. Jim all about my business.

"Have you ever heard of cupcakes for dogs?" I ask as soon as I get on the bus.

"No, can't say that I have," he replies.

"That's because I made them up," I tell him. "Ugly Brother loves them. Today I'm going to try them out on some other dogs."

"I'm a cat person," he mutters.

I pat his arm and smile. "It's okay if you like cats better," I say. What I don't tell him is that he gave me a great idea about cat cupcakes for later!

When I get off the bus, I wave to Mr. Jim with my beauty queen wave, nice and slow, side to side. He waves back.

Inside, Momma makes me change clothes. Once I pull on shorts and a T-shirt, I am ready to pack up a bag full of cupcakes. But as I'm riding my bike over to the shelter, I notice that Ugly Brother is tagging along.

"Just because you're comin' doesn't mean you can have another cupcake," I tell him. He whines, but keeps right on following me.

The Puppy Place is in an old mossy green house on River Street, down from the library.

The man who works at the shelter is Mr. Jay. His beard is gold like a lion, and he has a big laugh.

"Hi, Mr. Jay," I say. "I was wonderin' if it would be okay to give the doggies a treat today."

"What kind of treat, little miss?" he asks.

I explain all about my doggie cupcakes, and Mr. Jay smiles. "The pups will love getting a special treat," he says. "Follow me."

Ugly Brother and I follow him into the back of the house, where there is one big room with neat rows of cages along the walls. Right away, I notice the cutest little girl doggie named Countess. She is black and has a wrinkly face. I run over to get a closer look at her. She licks my hand.

"She's a sweetheart," Mr. Jay says. "I like to call her Tess."

I ask, "Can Tess come out of her cage to play with Ugly Brother?"

Mr. Jay lets her out. First Ugly Brother and Tess sniff each other a lot. Then they start playing with a pink chew toy.

While they play, Mr. Jay and I pass out cupcakes to all the sweet little doggies. The puppies love them. There's a wiener dog, a poodle, a lab, and a terrier.

"What kind of dog is Tess?" I ask.

"She is a Shar-Pei," Mr. Jay tells me. Then he sighs and adds, "I hate to do it, but I am going to have to close the Puppy Palace. I don't have enough money to keep it open."

I gasp. "Oh no! I hope all of these doggies get new homes soon!"

"They'll have to," Mr. Jay says. "I'm going to close in one week."

Ugly Brother puts his paws over his eyes and whines. This is terrible news. There has to be a way we can help.

Poor Ugly Brother hates to leave his new friend, but we promised to be back by dinnertime. Besides, I need to talk to Momma and Daddy about something important!

On the way home, I think about finding homes for all of those doggies. We could probably make sure the doggies there find new places to live, but if Mr. Jay closes, what happens if more dogs need help?

Slamming the door, I shout, "I need help!"

Everyone comes running. Momma asks, "Are you okay?"

"They are closing Puppy Place!" I cry. "We have to help Mr. Jay get enough money to stay open."

"Let's give the shelter our garage sale money," T.J. suggests.

"That's a great idea, son," Daddy says. "And my newspaper can run a story about the Puppy Place. Maybe it will get folks to donate."

I can't wait to tell Mr. Jay. I call him right up to say Daddy is going to put the shelter in the paper. He is so happy he hardly can talk. That's okay. I'm pretty good at talking, so I tell him all about our garage sale, too.

Mr. Jay is quiet for a minute after I tell him. Then he says, "You really do love dogs. Keeping the shelter open will save a lot of pups. They can't say thank you, but I am very grateful for any help your family can give us."

"Don't worry. Everything is going to be just fine. Goodbye for now," I tell him as I hang up.

Now it's really important for our sale to make a lot of money. Tomorrow when we get ready, we'll have to put higher prices on our old stuff. I sure hope folks will buy it all up.

Chapter Eight
Getting Ready

On Friday, I ask Cara, Paula, and Lucy to come home with me after school. My family is going to need help getting ready for the big sale. Our teacher lets us go to the office and use the phone during recess so they can get permission to ride the bus with me.

When Mr. Jim sees us all waiting at the bus door, he frowns and says, "Hold on just a minute! I see one girl who rides this bus and three who don't."

I smile my best dazzling beauty queen smile. Then I explain all about the dog shelter, the sale, and how we went to the office to use the phone. I can tell he wants me to finish talking, because his mouth is open like he wants to say something.

"Are you sayin' you have a note from the office that gives these girls permission to ride my bus today?" Mr. Jim says once I quit talking.

"Yes!" I say, throwing my hands up. "That's what I've been sayin'!"

By now there is a big long line behind us so we jump on the bus. I sit with Lucy. Cara and Paula sit across from us. We can't wait to get busy working. Before long, we pull up in front of my house. I see Daddy's truck in the driveway. He's home early to help, too!

Momma and Daddy are in the garage sorting things. Momma is the boss. She smiles when she sees us.

"Girls, you can make the signs and put the price tag stickers on things," she says. "T.J., bring out all those clothes from the hall closet so we can add them to the sale."

T.J. heads inside to grab the clothes. Momma has him hang them on the old clothesline beside the garage. Then she covers them with an old quilt.

"There's no chance of rain in the weather forecast," Daddy says.

"That's good," Momma says. "We don't want to have a rainy day sale. That would be just awful!"

My friends and I make the signs on white poster board squares. On each sign, we write GARAGE SALE in capital letters. Then we write my address in our best handwriting. Under that, we put the hours, 8 a.m. to 5 p.m.

I make little doggie faces and bones along the edges of my sign.

We make cupcake posters, too. Our posters are so cute. They have pink cupcakes with glitter on them and all the names and prices of the cupcakes.

T.J. walks by with his old sports gear for the sale. He tells us we should work more and talk less.

He just says that because he doesn't have anyone to talk to but Ugly Brother, who is following him around like a caboose on a choo-choo train.

Next, my friends and I use the pink stickers I picked out to make price tags. Lucy and I write the prices down, while Cara and Paula help Momma set things up on the tables.

Ugly Brother gets tired of helping T.J. and wanders over to me. I ask, "Are you goin' to help us now?"

He barks, "Ruff, ruff."

I give him a sheet of stickers to take to Momma. "Don't drool on these," I warn him. He gets one stuck on his nose. I laugh, pluck the sticker off, and tell him, "You're worth more than fifty cents!"

T.J. has a stack of video games he doesn't play anymore. "These are only worth fifty cents," he says. Paula starts putting the stickers on them right away.

"Stop!" I shout. "We should mark them a dollar. Remember, we're tryin' to save the doggies."

Paula says, "Right. I need some dollar stickers."

Daddy is selling his old stamp collection, some books, and some black boots with spurs on the backs. Momma thinks we can get a lot of money for the stamps and the boots. Books will only get fifty cents, but we put ten dollars on the boots.

I price my lemon cupcake cutie doll for five dollars. Momma marks the baby clothes, winter coats, Christmas ornaments, and my stuffed animals.

Ugly Brother wants to bring something to put in the sale, too! It's an ice-cream-cone chew toy, but he chewed the bottom right off and now it looks like a cupcake.

"Don't hurt his feelings," Lucy says. "Put it in the sale anyway."

I put twenty-five cents on it, but seeing that dog toy makes me think of that poor little girl dog at the shelter. I tell my friends all about Tess the dog. Then I add, "I sure hope she gets a family."

"Who do we know that needs a dog?" Paula asks.

Lucy shouts, "Miss Clarabelle!"

"That's right!" I say. "She said she gets lonely in her house. Tess would be perfect!"

Daddy always says that seeing is believing. If I bring Miss Clarabelle to the Puppy Place, seeing Tess will make her want to take that doggie home and keep her forever.

But that will have to wait until after the sale. Tonight, Momma's ordering us some pizza, and then we need to get lots of rest before the big day. All we have to do is wait until tomorrow. Hurry up, morning!

Chapter Nine
Garage Sale Heaven

The next morning, Momma wakes me up while it's still dark outside. Time to get my cupcakes ready!

After lining the cupcakes up on trays and piling them on stands, I carefully cover them with plastic wrap. I twirl it around and around so they will stay fresh.

Then I grab my little pencil bag with change in it, a notepad to write my sales on, and some brown paper lunch sacks to put the cupcakes in.

I set up right in front of the garage where everyone can see me. Kylie Jean Cupcakes is open for business!

People begin to arrive just as the sun comes up! Those garage sale customers are serious. Momma and Daddy don't even get any coffee. We are busy!

Soon, Miss Clarabelle comes over. "I just love Christmas decorations," she remarks, digging through a box.

I know I need to ask her about going to the Puppy Place. "Are you busy tomorrow after church?" I ask. "Because I want you to meet someone."

"Why, I'd love to meet a friend of yours," she tells me, smiling. "I'll see you right after church, then."

"Do you want to buy one of these scrumptious strawberry cupcakes?" I ask, holding up a cupcake.

She smiles again and says, "How can I refuse? They sound wonderful."

She pays me with a five-dollar bill. When I try to give her change back, she tells me I can keep it. Yay! I have some extra money for the puppies!

More of our neighbors and friends come to our sale. Daddy tells them we're donating the money we make to keep the dog shelter open. A lot of people tell us to keep the change for the dogs.

Every time someone walks up, I say, "Delicious cupcakes for sale! Get your cupcakes!"

Granny and Pappy arrive with donuts, coffee, and Lucy. They buy a dozen of my cupcakes! Ka-ching, ka-ching!

Then Lucy comes to help. Together we shout, "Delicious cupcakes for sale! Get your cupcakes here!"

I am pretty excited when my bus driver, Mr. Jim, comes by. He looks down at my table and says, "I'll take a dozen cupcakes. Did your momma help you bake them?"

"Yes, sir," I say, "and she is the best baker in Texas."

"They sure do look tasty," he says. "I don't think I can wait to eat one, so I'll have one right now." He chooses a red velvet cupcake and finishes it in two bites!

Mr. Jim looks around for a while and buys some of Daddy's old tools.

I think I am in garage sale heaven, but after lunchtime, it slows down. Lucy and I stand by the street with a cupcake sale sign, ready to wave at any cars that pass by. We don't see any.

At three o'clock, a lot of customers start coming again. I think these people are hoping to get a deal. Granny says that people like to offer less and they figure at the end of the sale you might just take less.

Cole, my friend from across the street, wanders over. He says, "Hey, y'all."

"Want to buy a cupcake?" I ask.

Cole looks at the cupcakes on my table. "Sure," he says. "But don't give me one with a dog bone on it."

There are only a few cupcakes on my table. There are a few dog cupcakes left, but every dog who tried them ate them right up. I'm glad I made them!

When five o'clock finally comes, we close the sale. It's time to clean up, but we're all tired. Garage sale days are long days!

There's still work to do. Daddy and T.J. put the leftover sale stuff in the back of the truck to go to the Goodwill store. Momma counts the money. Lucy and I help. We roll the coins.

Finally, Momma announces, "We made two hundred and twenty dollars and twenty-five cents for the Puppy Place!"

Lucy and I jump around and do a happy dance.

"Pretty good for a bunch of old stuff we didn't need anyway," Daddy says, smiling. "Kylie Jean can take a check over to the Puppy Place tomorrow after church."

"I hope it's enough to keep the shelter open until we can get more donations," Momma says. Then she looks at me. "We should figure out your profit," she says. When she sees my confused look, she explains, "A profit is how much money you made, not including the money you spent on supplies."

"How much did you spend at the Piggly Wiggly?" Daddy asks.

"About twenty dollars, I think," Momma says.

"And how much did you make at the sale?" Daddy asks me.

"I sold sixty-seven cupcakes!" I say proudly.

Daddy announces, "You made a forty-seven-dollar profit."

I smile. "That's a lot of money to bring to the doggie shelter," I say.

Ugly Brother really likes the idea. He barks, "Ruff, ruff!"

I'm tired from working hard all day, but my job isn't over. Now it's time to find a home for Tess.

Chapter Ten
Puppy Love

On Sunday afternoon, Miss Clarabelle comes over after church. "Who did you want me to meet, Kylie Jean?" she asks. "Is he or she here?"

"No," I tell her. "We have to go to the Puppy Place. I want you to meet my friend Mr. Jay."

"Oh, how nice," Miss Clarabelle says.

"Besides, I have to take the check and the doggie cupcakes to the shelter," I add. I don't tell her that secretly, I'm hoping she'll find a new puppy friend!

Ms. Clarabelle drives us over in her big white Cadillac. When we get there, the sign on the door says "open," so we go right in.

Mr. Jay looks up when we walk in. He says, "Well, hello, Miss Kylie Jean. How is our favorite patron today?"

I am puzzled. Frowning, I ask, "Can you please tell me what a patron is so I can answer your question?"

Mr. Jay laughs his big laugh. "A patron is a supporter," he says. "Someone who helps out. Just like you, helping out the Puppy Place."

"Oh!" I say. "Well, okay, I'm just fine and dandy. I brought my friend. We have something to give you, too."

Miss Clarabelle nudges me. "Please introduce me to your friend," she says quietly.

"Mr. Jay," I say, "This is my dear friend Miss Clarabelle."

"Pleased to meet you, ma'am," Mr. Jay says. He shakes her hand.

Then I hand him the envelope with the check and he opens it. He looks like a cat that just got a fresh fish dinner. He is so happy. "This is awesome!" he shouts. "With this money, we can stay open a little longer. Thank you so much, Kylie Jean."

"You're welcome," I say. "We're not givin' up, either. I want to raise some more money for you."

"That would be wonderful," Mr. Jay says.

Then I hear a quiet bark from the back room. That reminds me of the other reason we're here!

"Come on, Miss Clarabelle!" I say, grabbing her hand.

The puppies are all so cute. Miss Clarabelle and I stop at each cage. I tell her about each dog, and then we give them a doggie cupcake. They love them and eat them right up.

I save Tess's cage for last. When we get to her, she has a pink bow tied around her neck and looks so adorable. Mr. Jay lets her come out to play. Right away, the sweet little doggie gives Miss Clarabelle some sweet doggie kisses.

Miss Clarabelle sighs. "This is the prettiest, sweetest dog I've ever seen," she says.

I think it's love at first sight! "Her name is Tess," I tell her. "Short for Countess. I am so worried that Mr. Jay might not be able to find a home for her."

"That's true," Mr. Jay says. "She's the sweetest dog, but no one seems to want an older dog. Everyone just wants the puppies."

I can tell Miss Clarabelle is concerned. I say, "What if nobody wants her? Thinkin' about that makes me sadder than a hen without a chick."

Miss Clarabelle thinks for a minute. "You know," she says, "I get a little lonely in my big old house. If you could help me walk her sometimes, Kylie Jean, I think Tess could come and live with me."

I shout, "Hooray!"

Mr. Jay smiles. "You can fill out the adoption papers right now and take her home today," he says.

As soon as we're back at Miss Clarabelle's house, we sit on the front porch and watch Tess play in the yard. Ugly Brother knows I'm back, and he wants to see what's going on. He comes over. Right away, they start playing, and Ugly Brother licks Tess's ear.

I think that both Ugly Brother and Miss Clarabelle are falling in love with Tess!

I say, "Miss Clarabelle, I am so happy you decided to be Tess's new family. Now I can visit her all the time." Ugly Brother is happy, too. He comes over and licks Miss Clarabelle's hand.

"Are you trying to say thank you?" I ask.

Both of the doggies bark.

Ugly Brother barks, "Ruff, ruff!"

Tess barks, "Woof, woof!"

Two barks means yes!

Miss Clarabelle just pats Ugly Brother on the head. "You're welcome," she says.

The doggies sit on the steps together. They are so cute! Looking at them, I decide it must be puppy love!

Chapter Eleven
Out of Business

On Sunday night, our whole family is sitting at the supper table. The kitchen smells good, like chicken noodle soup.

Momma always makes soup when she is busy because it's easy. You put all of the ingredients in the pot and it cooks by itself.

Daddy asks, "Kylie Jean, when is your next sale going to be?"

"I'm all out of stuff to sell, but I can ask my friends," T.J. says.

"Don't worry," I say. "Granny and Pappy offered to have a sale so I can sell cupcakes."

Momma asks, "Are you ready to bake all of those cupcakes again? You still have a lot of them left over."

I reply, "Yup! Baking is fun."

Then Momma asks, "Guess what's for dessert?"

You guessed it — leftover cupcakes! They are sitting all over the kitchen counter like sweet little red and pink polka dots. I've had so many cupcakes that they don't even look good anymore. Maybe I don't want to be in the cupcake business after all.

Looking at all those leftover cupcakes, an idea hits me like sprinkles on a cupcake!

"How about a going-out-of-business sale?" I say.

Ugly Brother barks twice. That means yes!

And then we each eat one more cupcake.

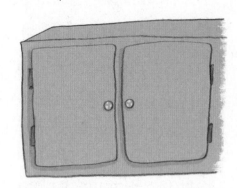

From Momma's Kitchen

PRINCESS CUPCAKES

YOU NEED:

1 box of your favorite cake mix (any flavor)

1 can of your favorite flavor frosting (not white)

sprinkles, colored sugar — whatever kinds you want!

1 tube of decorator's frosting, white color

cupcake liners in your favorite color

a muffin tin

Steps

1. Bake cupcakes as directed on your box of cake mix. (Make sure a grown-up helps you!)

2. Let cupcakes cool completely. Once the cupcakes cool, frost.

3. Using the decorator's frosting, draw a simple crown on each cupcake.

4. Use your sprinkles and colored sugar to fill in the crown.

Yum, yum!

From Momma's Kitchen

HONEY BEE SPELLING SURPRISE

YOU NEED:

Honey (1 tbsp per person)

Alphabet cereal (1/2 cup per person)

Plain or vanilla yogurt (8 oz per person)

Your favorite berries (1/4 cup per person)

1 clear glass for each person

Steps

1. Spoon honey into the bottom of each glass.

2. On top of the honey, add a layer of yogurt and a layer of berries. You can use thinner layers and repeat, or just do big thick layers.

3. On top of the yogurt and berries, add alphabet cereal. Finish with a drizzle of honey and a few more berries. Serve immediately.

Yum, yum!

Marci Bales Peschke was born in Indiana, grew up in Florida, and now lives in Texas with her husband, two children, and a feisty black-and-white cat named Phoebe. She loves reading and watching movies.

When **Tuesday Mourning** was a little girl, she knew she wanted to be an artist when she grew up. Now, she is an illustrator. She especially loves illustrating books for kids and teenagers. When she isn't illustrating, Tuesday loves spending time with her husband, who is an actor, and their children.